MEETING CHANCE

Visit us at www.boldstrokesbooks.com

By the Author

Andy Squared

Meeting Chance

MEETING CHANCE

by

Jennifer Lavoie

2013

MEETING CHANCE
© 2013 By Jennifer Lavoie. All Rights Reserved.

ISBN 10: 1-60282-952-7
ISBN 13: 978-1-60282-952-7

This Trade Paperback Original Is Published By
Bold Strokes Books, Inc.
P.O. Box 249
Valley Falls, NY 12185

First Edition: October 2013

Credits
Editors: Lynda Sandoval and Ruth Sternglantz
Production Design: Susan Ramundo
Cover Design By Sheri (graphicartist2020@hotmail.com)

Acknowledgments

There are many people who made this book possible, and without them, I wouldn't be writing this page at all. My eternal gratitude to Len Barot and the entire Bold Strokes Books team. Thank you for believing in me!

Thanks also to the World's Greatest Editor, Lynda Sandoval, for her patience and belief in Chance. These thanks extend to Sheri, Cindy, and Ruth, who were all important to making this book 100%.

To my students at MBMS, without whom this book may not have been written. And to my students at OCS, who helped me choose the final cover art for this book and learned a bit about the publishing world.

For all that they do to encourage reading and education: Pam Sloss, Toni Whitaker, R.E. Bradshaw, Cheryl Orahood, Laurie Lavoie, Yvonne Heidt, Barbara Wright, Ruth Sternglantz, Aleida Gonzalez, Karen Wolfer, Beth Schomburg, and anyone else who either remained anonymous or who I have forgotten unintentionally.

As always, to my family and friends, especially my parents and my siblings. I owe a huge debt to my coworker, Amy McCallum Bailey, who is the real life inspiration for the Amy in this book, and who answered whatever questions I had on fostering dogs. And a thank you to the real Megan and Brendan Corbin and their amazing Rottweilers.

Finally, to Alicia Wright and Melissa Zaluski from the Connecticut Humane Society in Newington, I thank you for taking time out of your busy day to speak with me about pit bulls, shelter procedures, and for the insightful tour of your wonderful facility.

If you or someone you know is looking to become a pet owner, please consider adopting from the Connecticut Humane Society. For more information visit www.cthumane.org

Dedication

For my students, who inspire me every day

CHAPTER ONE

The doors of the shelter in downtown Bristol loomed large before him. Despite the pouring rain, they were open beneath their maroon canopy. Aaron drummed his fingers on the steering wheel and stared at them through the rain-streaked window. He could wait a few more minutes. If he got out of his car now, he'd just get drenched, and then he'd be soaked for hours and smell worse than the dogs inside. What good would that do?

A few people came and went in the time he sat there, listening to the soft strains of music filter over his radio. Some of them noticed him, and he wondered what they thought of the teenager sitting in his beat-up car staring intently at the building. *They must think I'm a lunatic. Or a thief.*

The radio told him it was ten after four, and he knew he was late. His appointment with the director had been for four. Maybe he should just go home, call the woman—Maria, he remembered—and tell her he'd gotten caught up at school and couldn't make it. Maybe he could reschedule for another day.

Or never.

The two words were like a shock to him, racing straight through his spine. No. He would do this. He'd been planning it for a year now, and his mother would be so disappointed with him. He would be disappointed with himself.

He had just received his license two days ago, and his first major drive had been to the animal shelter, where he planned to change his life. For far too long he had lived in fear, but now everything would be different. He couldn't change the scars on his face, or the pain of the memories, but he could change other things.

If only he could get out of the car.

A moment later, the rain eased up and Aaron forced himself from the ripped cloth of his car seat. He trotted to the front door, lingering a moment under the canopy as he pushed his hair back and stepped into the glowing interior of the shelter.

The scent of bleach hit him first, followed by the softer and somehow sharper scent of dog. A large orange feline lounged on the desk in front of him, not even bothering to pick up its head when he placed one hand on the counter. He would have thought it was fake if the whiskers hadn't twitched.

The woman behind the desk looked up and smiled briefly. "Can I help you?"

"My name is Aaron Cassidy. I have an appointment with the director."

The woman pushed a stack of papers off a large desk calendar and ran her finger down until it stopped on that date. "Ah, yes. You were scheduled to meet with her at four."

"Yes, I ran a little late," he said, despite his car being clearly visible through the open doors. "If she's busy, I can reschedule if that's better."

The woman picked up the phone, hit a single button, and held up a "one moment" finger.

Aaron reached out while she talked on the phone and ran a hand across the cat's fur. She picked her head up and looked at Aaron, and he realized she was large because of a swollen, pregnant belly. She purred loudly and settled back into her nap just as the woman put down the handset.

"Maria said to go on into her office. It's around the corner to your right, first door."

"Thanks." He followed her directions and found the door wide open. A woman sat behind a large desk, seeming to not even notice two kittens rolling around on a pile of papers, sending the stack all over the place. Aaron knocked timidly on the door frame.

"Come in, Aaron," Maria said, looking up with a smile. She glanced at the clock. "I expected you at four," she added, picking up one kitten up and setting it on a small bed on the floor.

"I'm sorry," Aaron started, about to give her the same excuse he'd given the other woman, but he stopped short. It probably wouldn't be a good idea to lie to the woman he wanted to work for. "I was nervous," he finally admitted.

"Based on what you told me over the phone, it is understandable," she said as her brown eyes flickered toward the scar that ran the length of Aaron's face.

He knew how he looked with the scar that ran in a jagged line from the corner of his lip to his chin. Not to mention the puncture wounds by his right eye that nearly connected with the one on his lip. When he offered her a smile, there was an uneven quirk that the doctors hadn't been able to fully correct. He would live with those scars for the rest of his life, and he wasn't yet an adult. Wait—Maria had been talking to him, and he hadn't heard a word of it. "I'm sorry, what did you—?"

"Aaron? Are you sure you want to do this?"

He nodded after a moment. "I'm sure. I've wanted to since last year. I *need* to do this."

Maria smiled and stood, reaching across the desk to shake his hand. "You're a brave young man. I'm sure you'll do fine here. Happy Endings Animal Foundation has a wonderful staff of volunteers, and you'll fit in just fine. We have quite a few animals running around, but they are separated. Why don't I give you a tour of the facilities first, and then we can get you your first assignment."

"What would that be?"

"We will definitely start you gradually. I know you're eager to get over your fear, but I'm not going to throw you to the dogs, so to speak."

Aaron laughed awkwardly with her.

"Based on your application, you'll work with the cats first. Get acclimated to the environment. The dogs are in the next room, and believe me, you'll hear them. They can be very energetic."

"What sorts of dogs do you take in?"

"Oh, we get many different breeds. Some of them are strays or animals that were dropped off by owners who could no longer keep them. It's sad, but it happens more often than you would think in this economy."

"Do you get abused animals?"

Maria frowned. "Unfortunately, yes. Sometimes. But we only take animals that we believe we can adopt out. We are a limited euthanasia shelter. Any animal that comes here stays until they find a good home, if possible. We have made very few exceptions to this rule."

"What exceptions have there been?" Aaron asked, curious.

"Well, sometimes we get an animal that appears fine but has severe health issues that impact the quality of their life. Most illnesses can be helped with medication, but there have been a few cases where the animal will not survive, and to prevent further suffering we do the humane thing."

The director led Aaron down the hall, back in front of the reception area, to a locked hallway and let them in. Cats lounged in large cages and on top of them. Two closed doors lined up on the right side, with large observation windows in the wall beside them. Another two doors on the left side of the hallway were labeled *kennels*, and one long, tall window looked into that room. Aaron could see more cats lazing in cages.

"We've had to turn away dogs before, but if we catch wind they're going to one of *those* shelters…well, we make room somehow. Anyway, this is the cattery as you can see. Cats everywhere! Many of them are free to roam if they want, for at least a few hours a day. Watch out for some of them, though. They'll try to sneak out. Like this guy over here, Spitball."

Maria pointed to a gray cat with a large white circle on its forehead. It mewed loudly when it saw her. Aaron laughed. The name sounded horrible, but it really looked like a spitball had been launched at the center of its forehead and stuck to the fur.

"Who named him that?"

"My son," Maria sighed. "He's five. Where he learned what a spitball is, I have no idea. But once he named him, he cried whenever we called him something else. So it stuck." Her lips quirked. "No pun intended."

"What are these rooms for?" he asked, pointing to two adjacent doors. Maria led him over and gestured through the window. Cages were placed in aisles, stacked three high to the ceiling and many deep. The room was a warm yellow orange with pictures of kittens and their mothers in frames on the wall.

"This room is our maternity ward, for the expectant mothers and their kittens. You won't be working in here, though. Not for a while. We reserve this room for the senior staff. It's a lot of work to handle the newborns, and we like to make sure they're in the best hands possible. After the first few days, we usually have a foster family come and pick them up to give them more attention in a home setting." She brought him over to the next window. Inside, more aisles of cages lined the wall and the lights were dim. "This is quarantine for the sick cats. Usually it's an upper respiratory infection, which is highly contagious. We keep them separated until they're healthy so they won't infect the others, especially the pregnant cats. If you have to go in here at any point always wash up after and before touching any other animal. However, if you're assigned duty to this room, it's likely that you won't work anywhere else on your shift." She gestured to the hand sanitizer on the wall and the bucket on the floor. In it sat a towel, soaked with bleach. A sign next to it read, "Please wash your shoes after leaving."

"Makes sense," Aaron agreed. A door at the end of the hall opened, and the din of dogs barking filled the air. Only one of the cats seemed affected and dove for cover. Aaron felt like joining it under the cage, but he knew it wouldn't make the best impression. *There isn't any room for me under there, anyway.*

"And that would lead to our dog kennels," Maria said as she started toward it. A guy about Aaron's age stood in the doorway, holding a clipboard. "It's set up more or less like this room. There's a maternity ward for pregnant dogs, but we never have as many as we do cats, and the quarantine room is larger, obviously. All of the dogs are crated or kenneled as well, unless they're being supervised. The last door to your left in this hallway leads to our storage area. It also opens up into the dog kennels."

"Maria, I need your help with the shepherd. He needs a bath and he's being stubborn. Do you have a few minutes?"

"Sure. Aaron, this is Finn. He volunteers after school on Fridays and the weekends, just like you'll be doing."

"Hey," Finn said, grinning at him. His brown hair fell over his forehead, almost—but not quite—hiding eyes that were an even darker brown. He was taller than Aaron by a few inches.

"Hey," Aaron returned, reaching up self-consciously and brushing his red hair forward. The tips covered the scars by his eyes.

"You want to help out with Prince? He's a pain to get in the bath, but he's a lot of fun. Then I can take over tour duties and show you the clinic and groom room."

Aaron's heart skipped a beat and his muscles locked, preventing him from moving. He stared at Finn, who looked at him expectantly. At his hairline, tiny beads of sweat formed and worked their way down the side of his face. The din of the barking dogs had nothing on the beat of his heart, slamming against his ribcage.

After tense moments of silence, Maria stepped in for him. "He's going to get used to handling the cats first. We don't want Prince getting slobber all over him the first day he's here." She turned to Aaron. "Prince is a handful. Would you like to see the dogs?" she asked quietly.

"No, that's okay," he said, reaching out to pet a black ball of fur. "I'll just stay and get to know some of the cats." *One step at a time*, he thought, concentrating on slowing his racing heart. *Just coming here today was a big first step.*

"Okay. I'll be back in a few minutes and see how you're doing. If you want to, just play with them for a while. I'll send Finn over to show you the ropes when we're finished."

"Nice meeting you, Aaron. I'm sure we'll have a blast together." Finn waved over his head as he walked back into the dog room. Maria shut the door behind her and the sounds of the dogs faded into the background.

Aaron was left alone with the cats. Most of them dozed in cages while some older kittens tumbled with each other on the floor in a large pen, and one ancient-looking cat watched him lazily from a perch up in the corner.

"Hello," he said, walking over to it. He reached up, stretching to the cat's perch and barely touching the top. The cat sniffed him then squeaked. He wasn't sure if it was a good sound or not, so he backed off and sat on the floor. One of the kittens ambled over to him and poked his paw through the pen. Aaron lifted him out and set him down. He batted at the laces on his shoes. Aaron laughed and played with him, picking him up and rolling him onto his back. His body was gray, but the tip of his tail looked like it had been dunked in black ink. "You're adorable," he said when it crawled into his lap and curled up. Before he realized what was happening, the kitten had fallen asleep.

There were so many adorable cats around. If it were up to him, he would take them all home, but he knew his mother wouldn't be too thrilled. They already had one cat, and according to her, one was enough. But this ball of fluff in his lap looked too cute. He didn't know what it had been named, but Inky looked like it would fit.

The door to the dog kennels opened and Finn stepped through. His eyes fell on Aaron sitting on the floor and he grinned. "Isn't he the sweetest? People have been looking at him all week. He just went up for adoption. He'll find a great home really soon, I'm sure."

"Oh," Aaron said, feeling disappointed. He had wanted to sneak him home. "Does he have anyone asking for him yet?"

"Well, all potential families go through a screening process. The two that put in for him were turned down. They already had multiple-cat homes. Maria doesn't mind adopting out to homes like that, but when there are too many cats in one home, she gets anxious. She worries that they won't get the attention they deserve."

"Oh, well that's good. I mean, I hope he gets a home and all."

Finn flopped down next to him, lounging on his side as he reached out and played with the kitten's tail. "Why, are you interested?"

"Maybe, but we already have a cat and my mom would say no."

"Would she? You don't know until you ask."

Aaron shrugged. "What's his name?"

"Little Dipper." He laughed. "Because it looks like he dipped his tail in a can of paint."

"I like it," Aaron agreed, laughing with him. "I was thinking Inky might be a cute—I mean cool—name for him."

"Inky is cute. Maybe whoever adopts him will change his name. It happens all the time. But enough lying around and playing. We've got work to do."

Aaron set Little Dipper on the ground and stood. He hated to leave him behind, but Finn was right. He had come here for a reason, and it couldn't be all fun and games.

CHAPTER TWO

Aaron had to change litter boxes as his first job at the shelter; he did it at home all the time, so he didn't mind the smell, but the litter was different here. Instead of sand-like material, the litter came in the form of little pellets made from recycled newspaper. It made less mess than at home, and he considered switching his cat's litter as soon as he ran out of the current brand.

Working with Finn made the time pass quickly, and Aaron found himself completely at ease around him. Because of his scarred face and the reactions it drew from people, he usually had a hard time connecting with others, so it surprised him when he found himself chatting easily with Finn.

"You should come to the bookstore and see me after school sometime. I work there Monday through Wednesday until eight."

"How do you manage it? I mean, school, volunteering, and a job? How are your grades?"

Finn offered a sheepish grin. "I made the honor roll last marking period."

Aaron gaped at him in amazement. He struggled to keep his grades up and didn't have a steady job. "You're superhuman. I couldn't do it."

"You could do it if you wanted to badly enough," Finn said with a shrug. "My parents don't have a lot of money, so I need to save for college. And I have the worst car imaginable. It barely runs, so I need to get it fixed all the time. But I guess it's not so bad. It could be worse."

"Why do you volunteer if you need the money for school? Wouldn't it make more sense to just concentrate on working?" Aaron closed the last cage and moved to put the scooper away while Finn tied up the old litter in a bag.

"I want to be a vet. If I volunteer, it gives me a reference for my college applications. Whatever school takes me will know I'm serious, too. Plus if I'm going to school for veterinary medicine, I can be a volunteer vet tech here."

"That makes sense." He couldn't argue the logic and put his hands on his hips to wait for his next instructions.

Not for the first time since they had started working together, Finn's eyes darted quickly to the scars on his face. Aaron had to repress the sigh that built in his chest. "Go ahead. I know you want to ask."

"I'm sorry," Finn muttered, glancing away. "I didn't mean to stare."

"Most people don't. I know—it looks pretty bad. But it's a lot better than it was before. And no, it doesn't hurt me anymore." *Except on some days when the scar tissue feels tight and pulls at my face.*

"What happened?"

Aaron closed his eyes for a moment. Every single time he told the story, he relived it. People told him the memories would fade with time, but that wasn't the case. The attack happened seven years ago and the visions were as fresh as if it had happened just yesterday. "When I was nine, our neighbors had a Dalmatian. It was a good dog, I guess, but it always wanted to play and didn't know when to stop. One day, I was riding my bike in the street and the dog got out of the backyard. I don't know how it did, but it came tearing out and chased me. I thought it just wanted to play, so I rode in circles and teased him. He barked like he usually did and jumped around. I slowed down a little to reach out and pet him, but when I did that, he snapped. He lunged at me and knocked me off my bike. My head hit the ground, but I had my helmet on. Maybe he wanted the straps from the helmet—I don't know. I felt his teeth sink into my face and he snarled. I screamed for my mom and she came running. I couldn't get the dog off me."

"What did your mom do?" Finn asked, a look of horror crossing his face.

"She got him off somehow. I couldn't see because I was bleeding so badly and trying to keep him from biting me more. She picked me up and ran for the house. My dad called for an ambulance and I remember part of the ride to the hospital, and then nothing."

"I'm so sorry. That…it must have been horrible."

Aaron offered a weak laugh. "You have no idea. I've been afraid of dogs ever since."

"If you're afraid of dogs, why are you volunteering here?"

"I guess I don't want to be afraid anymore. The fear is…too big a part of my life. Everyone I know has dogs. I can't hang out with my friends without sweating and shaking every time I see a dog or hear one barking in the backyard. I'm tired of it. I decided I needed to do this."

Finn smiled. "You're a pretty tough guy, you know that?"

"Tough," Aaron said, with a scoff. "I can't even walk into the dog room. That's not tough in my book."

"Yes, but most people would either live with it or just go to therapy. But you're facing it and giving back at the same time."

Aaron tilted his head, hands shoved deep in his pockets. "You know, I never thought of it that way." He returned Finn's smile with one of his own.

"Well, stick with me and you'll get over your fear in no time. I love dogs. Can't have one in the apartment we live at, but I get my fix of them here. It's sad to see the ones you get attached to get adopted. I mean, it's great because they're going to a good home, but at the same time you'll probably never see them again."

"You mean like Inky—I mean, Little Dipper?"

Finn nodded. "Yeah. Exactly. It's hard when you first start. I would warn you not to get too attached like my mentor told me, but I know you won't listen."

"What do you mean I won't listen? I'm listening now, aren't I?"

"I didn't mean it that way. Of course you'll listen. But even if I tell you not to, it's going to happen anyway. It's impossible not to get attached. Just don't expect the kittens to stay here forever. They go the quickest because no one can resist them. If you're lucky, the owners will update us with pictures, but that's about it."

Aaron shrugged. "I'll do my best."

"Just looking out for you," Finn said.

The rain had finally stopped when Aaron pulled into the driveway and parked next to his mother's car. The lights were on in the kitchen, and a warm glow covered the front porch. Though exhausted, both physically and emotionally, pride coursed through Aaron. He had not gone near the dogs, but he had been in the building with them. He could hear them on the other side of the door, and after some time, he'd even relaxed. Being with Finn put him at ease. He just had one of those likeable personalities. It didn't hurt that he was hot, too, with dark eyes and hair that half hid his eyes to make him look mysterious.

"I'm home," he announced when he walked in the front door. Immediately he removed his shoes and put them on the shoe rack. A sweet scent drifted through the house and teased his stomach. "Something smells great!" he called when his first comment got him no response.

The house was suspiciously quiet, so he made his way to the kitchen. "Mom? Are you home?" The lights in the kitchen were all on, and a small cake sat on the counter with a candle stuck in it, lit, with the wax dripping onto the frosting.

"Surprise!" came the shout from behind him, and he spun. His mother stood in the doorway, her face brighter than the candle on the cake. "Congratulations on your first day! How did it go?"

Aaron smiled. Mom had always been so supportive of him, and it made him happy to know she'd be there for him, no matter what. "It went well. I got to work with the cats."

"Well, blow out the candle! We'll have a piece of cake and talk about it."

"What's the candle for? It's not my birthday."

"No," she agreed, "but it is a momentous day for you. I thought the cake would make it even better."

Aaron blew out the candle and sat while his mother sliced the cake. She joined him at the table and they dug in while he told her about Maria, Finn, and the cats.

"There's this really cute kitten, Mom. They call him Little Dipper because his tail looks like he stuck it in a can of paint. I called him Inky, though. He's really sweet and needs a good home…"

His mother sighed and put down her fork. "Aaron, we've already talked about this. We can't really afford another animal, and Midnight's getting older. I don't think he would like some little thing running around his space. Besides, you just started working there."

"Mom, please? Just come and look at him. He's so friendly. And he's with so many other cats, I'm sure he'd get along with Midnight just fine!"

"Him getting along with Midnight isn't the problem. It's Midnight getting along with him. Look, sweetheart, I'm sure he's a great cat, but you know money is tight since dad left…"

Aaron hung his head and nodded. "I know, I'm sorry. I just thought…since we already have a cat, the litter wouldn't be much more. They could share a box and the food…Midnight doesn't eat much, as it is."

"The food and the litter we could manage. But the vet bills are something different. The last time Midnight got sick it cost a lot of money. What if this kitten isn't healthy?"

Once again, his mother had a point. Aaron couldn't argue with her, but he still felt disappointed. Maybe he could ask about getting a job.

The phone rang and his mom reached over to answer it. "Hello?" she said as Aaron took a bite of his cake. She paused and shot him a glance. "Hi, Richard. Yes, he's home now. I'll let him tell you about it." She handed the phone over to him and picked up her cake. "It's your father. I'll let you talk to him in private."

Aaron took the phone. "Hi, Dad?"

"Hey, bud. How was the shelter today? I called earlier but Mom said you were still there. You hang in there all right?"

He smiled and nodded though his dad couldn't see him. "Yeah, it was okay. I worked with the cats. This other kid, Finn, showed me around the place."

"Did you get to the dogs?"

"No, not yet. They told me I could get comfortable with the cats first, and then they'd slowly work me up to the dogs."

"That's great news. I'm really proud of you, son."

"Thanks, Dad." Even though his parents divorced three years ago, he could still count on his father being there for him. He felt lucky. Some of his friends didn't have one or the other parent in their life because the divorce had been messy. His parents both cared about him enough to keep their personal relationship out of their relationships with him. Because of that, he got to see them both, sometimes together. But he never once thought about them getting back together. He could see they were much happier without each other, and that was okay with him.

"So you and this Finn kid…you get along all right?"

"Yeah, he's cool. He told me to visit him when he's working at the bookstore."

"Sounds like someone who could be a real friend. Does he know?"

"About what? The attack? Yeah, kind of hard to miss it, Dad. He asked what happened and I told him. Once he knew he stopped looking at my scars. I don't think he'll have a problem if I, you know, freak out a little bit around the dogs." Aaron laughed quietly.

His father sighed on the other end of the line. "That's good. You need more friends like that, Aaron. People who won't judge you for any reason."

Aaron knew the true meaning behind his words and nodded to himself. After he had been attacked and his fear of dogs started, most of the other kids seemed to understand. His friends Tyler and Caleb didn't completely get it, but they seemed to accept him, even if they were a little wary. However, as they grew older and entered high school they told him to man up and get over it.

Their judgment got even worse when he came out to them the year he had turned fifteen. He'd expected some resistance to the idea of his being gay, but they'd been friends for so long, he'd hoped they could get over it and support him like his parents had. But with each week that passed, they seemed to grow more distant. They started to do things without including him and then mention it in passing, after the fact. When he thought about it, he realized he couldn't really call them friends anymore. He didn't even remember the last time they had hung out together without his sexuality being brought up.

"Does he know about the other thing?"

"Dad," he replied with a roll of his eyes. "I don't just come out and say, *Hey, my name is Aaron, I'm afraid of dogs and I'm gay,* to every person I meet."

His father chuckled. "Okay, you're right. I guess that would be strange."

Aaron appreciated the fact that his dad at least tried to talk about his queerness. He was just so…awkward about the whole thing.

"I'm sure it will come out some time. It always does."

"Well, if he understands the dog issue, I'm sure he'll be fine with the other thing."

"Yeah." Because those two things were so similar. Not.

"Is there anything else you want to talk about?" Dad pressed.

Aaron hesitated before launching into the story of Inky. He glanced at the door to the kitchen, feeling guilty about it like a four-year-old kid who stole candy from the store. But he really did want that kitten. His father listened quietly as he explained everything.

"Sounds like a sweet animal. I'm proud of the work you're doing, Aaron. Keep it up, okay?"

"Okay."

"Can I talk to Mom for a minute?"

"Sure," he said, perking up. "Mom?" he called through the doorway. She appeared a moment later, Midnight trotting in after her, licking his lips like he'd just had some frosting. "Dad wants to talk to you." She frowned but took the phone with her out of the room.

Aaron struggled to hear what she was saying but gave up. He used his fork to pull the frosting off the cake to save it, then ate the cake and slowly licked the remaining frosting from the fork. He carefully scraped it against the plate to get every last piece of it off.

When his mother returned a few minutes later he glanced up at her and tried to keep the guilt from his face. She sighed. "Aaron, sometimes I don't know what I'm going to do with you."

He smiled sheepishly. "I don't know either, Mom."

"What time does the shelter open tomorrow? We'll go take a look at this kitten. Your father seems to think it'll be a good thing for you. He's agreed to pay for the vet bills if we'll take care of everything else."

Aaron stared at his mom in amazement and then jumped up to hug her. "Thank you!" He hadn't been expecting that reaction from either of them, even if he'd secretly hoped for it.

"Thank your father, not me. He can still be persuasive when he wants to be. I just hope he comes through on those vet bills."

"Dad's always paid, Mom. You know that. If he says he'll do something, he will."

"Well, we'll see. Besides, your kitten might already be adopted."

Aaron crossed his fingers behind his back, hoping that wasn't the case. "Finn said people were looking at him but weren't approved. He'll still be there."

CHAPTER THREE

Even though it was Saturday, Aaron managed to get his mother out of the house early, and they arrived at the animal shelter shortly after it opened. He hadn't been able to sleep half the night in the excitement of getting the cat, and he didn't want to get there too late to show Inky to his mom and get the paperwork started. At a quarter after ten they pulled into the parking lot and slipped into the front door. Aaron waved at the receptionist, Sandra, and asked if Maria was available.

"She's with a family right now, finishing adoption papers. She'll be out in a few minutes if you want to wait."

He nodded. "We'll wait. We're here to fill out some papers, too." He grinned. She smiled back at him.

"I'll let her know she has an appointment, then."

"Thanks. Is Finn here yet?"

"Got here about an hour ago," Sandra said, leaning back in her chair. "He'll be working until five. He's out back walking the dogs if you want to see him."

Aaron wanted to, but he also didn't want to bother him while he took care of the dogs. "That's okay," he said, swallowing roughly. "I'll wait."

Sandra shrugged as she picked up the phone and let Maria know she had a family looking to adopt. As she hung up the phone, she waved toward him and his mother. "She said she'd be out in five minutes. Just have a seat."

"You're sure you want to do this?" his mom asked, sitting next to him in a hard plastic chair. "You can't do this every time you find a cute animal, and you just started here."

"Yes, I'm sure. You'll love the kitten, Mom. He's really sweet."

"I'm sure I will. All kittens are sweet. It's when they grow older and turn into cats like Midnight that they're a problem," she said, amused.

A few minutes later they stood up when Maria walked into the room. She escorted a family with a cat carrier and shook their hands before they left.

"Aaron! It's good to see you, but your shift doesn't start until two."

Aaron's body shook as his excitement grew. "I know, but I'm here with my mom about an adoption." He felt like he was five again, picking out Midnight from the litter at some woman's house.

Maria's lips turned up pleasantly and she shook his mother's hand. "An adoption? Well, isn't that soon? Fell in love with one of the little furballs, did you? Let's see what we can do, then. You know there's a process that we go through, but I can see about expediting the paperwork." She led them to the cats. "Which particular feline was it?"

"Ink—ah, Little Dipper," Aaron said, still nervously excited. "I told Mom all about him last night and Finn said families already looked at him so I wanted to move fast."

Maria slowed as she entered the room and turned to look at him, the smile gone from her face. "Oh, Aaron…I'm so sorry. The adoption that just left was Little Dipper. I called them last night to approve them."

Aaron's heart sank. *So this is what Finn meant about getting close to the animals. I should have listened to him.* He hadn't realized disappointment would come so soon or so sharply. Mom squeezed his shoulder. "Finn said the people looking already had cats…"

"Finn likes to think he knows everything that goes on here, but he doesn't. He doesn't see all the paperwork that comes in. I know he wants to do more work around here, but I'll have to keep him out of my office." Maria frowned. "Was there someone else that caught your interest?"

"No, it was just him. He was so sweet yesterday."

"Yes, he was a sweetheart. He won over the staff and quite a few families, too. He's going to a good home, Aaron, I promise. He'll be well cared for, and they've promised to send pictures. I know it isn't the same thing, but you'll get to see how he's doing."

He nodded, but a hollow pit formed in his stomach. "Thanks. Sorry for taking up your time."

"Are you sure you didn't want to look for another cat? They have so many," his mother said, gesturing to the cats lounging around the room. "I'm sure they have other kittens, too, if that's what you really wanted."

"Thanks, but I was only interested in Dipper."

His mother frowned but nodded. "Maybe it was for the best. Who knows, maybe another cat will come in that will catch your attention and need you even more."

Aaron felt grateful that his mom tried to make him feel better, and he nodded, but he knew that wouldn't be the case. Nothing could win him over like that little kitten had.

❖

Returning to the shelter at two was difficult after the morning's disappointment, but Aaron made sure he didn't arrive late. He greeted Sandra for the second time that day and checked in with Maria, then went to look in on the cats. Finn stood in the room, changing towels in the cages.

"Hey, I heard you came in for Dipper this morning," he said as Aaron pulled out a clean stack of towels and placed them next to him without looking over. "I told you not to get attached, man."

"But I came to adopt him. I didn't think he'd be gone so fast."

"Yeah, well, I'll give you that one. I didn't think so either. I thought for sure Maria would turn them down, but I guess I spoke too soon." Finn shrugged. "What are you gonna do." He rubbed the ears of the cat in the cage before shutting the door. "But it's a good learning experience, right? At least you'd only played with the kitten for one day. It's not like he'd been here for weeks and you had a bond. That's the worst."

Aaron nodded absently and let Finn ramble as he worked next to him. Finn folded the towels precisely before changing out the old with the new. He checked the tag on each cage, and if it had only been a day since the last change, and the towel or bedding was clean, he left it. The old, dirty towels he tossed into the laundry basket on the floor as he moved down the line of cages. He made every fold in a way so the blanket or towel covered the entire sleeping area. Despite himself, Aaron watched and slowly relaxed, helping with movements that weren't nearly as sure as Finn's. The cages that had been changed had the markers snapped off and replaced with new ones, specifying the day of the week.

An hour passed and they lapsed into a companionable silence. Soon all the cages were changed, and Aaron picked up the laundry basket of towels.

"I can help you take your mind off Dipper if you'd like," Finn finally said. Aaron glanced up and found him leaning against the wall, arms crossed in front of his chest.

"How?"

"What do you say to starting with the dogs today? With the puppies," Finn amended. "They do like to nibble, I'll warn you, but they don't have the strength in their jaws to bite. So you don't have to be afraid, okay?"

Aaron looked at him with a steady frown to cover his suddenly racing pulse. Without answering he passed by him and pushed out of the room and into the next to load the washer. Finn followed him.

Cold beads of sweat started to form on his forehead, and he felt one roll down the side of his face. If his body reacted like this at just the thought of it, could he really do this? *I've only been here one day! Finn is insane.* "I thought only senior volunteers were allowed to work with the puppies and kittens." He shoved a bunch of the towels into an open washer and closed it. He started it on a new cycle and then moved to one that had finished in order to switch the wet blankets into the dryer.

"Before you came in today, I got permission from Maria. She's cool with it. Besides, you're a special case. She understands that you need to start slowly and work your way up."

"Being with the dogs on my second day isn't very slow," Aaron argued.

"No, it's not, but you're starting slow by starting small!" Finn laughed, leaning against one of the dryers.

"I don't want her to bend the rules for me. Then everyone will expect it." It was an excuse, he knew, but he wasn't ready; he knew that much, too.

"Nah, it's cool I tell you. Everyone will understand. Come on."

Finn grabbed his wrist gently and led him out of the storage room and directly into the dog wing. The dogs' loud barking instantly increased, and Aaron cringed. His heart slammed against his chest painfully and his breathing hitched as they passed by all the cages. He tried to slow his breathing, but he feared he would start to hyperventilate if he didn't get out of there soon. Twisting his hand, Aaron grabbed Finn's wrist. His fingers clutched him. If it hadn't been for that lifeline, Aaron would have run.

The door to the maternity room was shut, and Finn opened it carefully even though all the dogs in this room, like the main room, were in cages and crates. Two of the cages had sleeping puppies larger than the others, with no visible mother.

Despite his lightheadedness and concern for his own safety, his curiosity was piqued. "Where are the mothers?" he asked.

"With the huskies, the mother was hit by a car and killed."

"Wow. Sad."

Finn nodded. "We've been caring for them since they were about three weeks old. Someone brought them in, and a volunteer fostered them until last week." He flicked a hand toward another kennel. "The Rottweiler puppies were found abandoned. We don't know what happened to the mother. They're about nine weeks old, we think, based on their size and development."

Finn gestured to the dispenser on the wall and they both sanitized their hands.

Aaron had to admit that the dogs looked so sweet lying there in quiet heaps of fluffy fur.

"Do they have names?"

"No, not yet. Mostly they're referred to as the pups." Finn opened the cage with the huskies and pulled out the one that picked up his head. "They don't need to be bottle-fed anymore, so their foster family brought them back to be adopted out."

He held the puppy out to Aaron. They looked at each other, Aaron skeptically and the puppy with a look of tired boredom. He yawned, emitting a low squeak. With trembling hands, Aaron reached out, fingers sinking into the soft white fur and grasping the warm body beneath it. He felt the puppy's racing pulse and the tiny body breathing.

Finn smiled encouragingly and shifted closer to him to make sure he didn't drop the fragile creature.

"He's fuzzy," Aaron whispered. Finn nodded and pressed the puppy securely into Aaron's arms. It felt almost like holding a baby. Except for the fur. Finn stood so close their feet were touching, and Aaron's heart raced for another reason. Since he'd come out to his friends, not one of them had gotten close like this, even if they were fooling around with a football after school. As if they were afraid he'd try something with them. If Finn knew, would he keep his distance like Tyler and Caleb?

Distracted by his thoughts, he didn't notice when the puppy stretched up to his face and sniffed at him. A tiny tongue darted out and licked his cheek, and Aaron jumped.

"Easy," Finn said softly, placing a hand under the puppy. Aaron didn't want to drop him, but he hadn't been expecting that. "See? Not so bad."

"When they're small, maybe," Aaron reluctantly agreed. *This is okay. I can do this. A little guy isn't so bad. And he is sort of cute.* But the bigger dogs were out of the question. Still, despite his reassurances to himself, his palms sweated and his pulse continued to race. Any longer and he'd pass out.

"We can stay with the puppies as long as you need until your confidence grows."

Aaron jerked his head up to look at him. "You don't expect me to move on to the bigger dogs today, do you?"

Finn shook his head. "No, of course not. We have plenty of time. And a lot of work to get done, too. Always work to do around here."

"I feel like you're going to work me harder than Maria would."

"Of course! If I don't work you hard, I'll have to do it all myself."
Finn grinned and Aaron noticed the dimple in his left cheek for the
first time. His face heated and he glanced down at the puppy.

"I thought you liked working."

"I do, don't get me wrong. But when I can share the work with
someone else, what's the point in breaking my back, right?" Finn took
the puppy from him and placed him back in the cage with his brothers
and sisters. Aaron breathed a sigh of relief and wiped his palms on
his jeans. "Hey, so I get off work at five today. You're working until
six, right? Did you want to maybe get something to eat? Hang out or
something?"

"But you'd be hanging around for an hour."

Finn shrugged and pushed his hair back. "I can go home and
get changed, then come back and get you. Or you could meet me
somewhere."

Aaron tensed, unsure of the protocol in this situation. *Finn is
a good guy, a friend, who wants to hang out. I should go, right?* He
frowned, and the tightness of the scars pulled at his lip. When had he
last hung out with the guys? He could hardly even remember, it had
been so long. They were cool with the scars but the whole "gay thing"
as they called it…that was another story. If Finn knew, would he
change his mind, too? Did Aaron want to lose another friend simply
because of who he was? *Or am I being ridiculous and judging Finn
because of how Caleb and Tyler reacted?*

"I don't know…"

His mentor tilted his head to the side, hair falling back into his
face as he glanced down at him. The difference in height wasn't that
significant, but at that moment Aaron felt it. "What's wrong, Aaron?
We won't go anywhere fancy if that's what you're worried about.
I can barely afford it myself, but I thought it would be cool. To be
honest, I don't get to hang out with others much because of school,
work, and volunteering here. My friends at school don't exactly keep
the same hours I do."

"Money isn't the issue," he said, shoving his hands in his back
pockets. He hesitated. "I guess we could go…if you want to."

"Yeah, it'll be cool. We won't get to really talk much here without
interruption unless it's about the animals, you know?"

"Or answering to Maria barking out orders." Aaron laughed.

"So true. We on for later? Do you want to meet somewhere or should I come get you?"

"I'll drive," Aaron said quickly. There was a family restaurant just down the road that had good but cheap food. "Gracie's Restaurant?"

"Sounds great. They have awesome burgers. I'll meet you there at six thirty, unless you want to go home and change."

Aaron shook his head. "No, that's okay. Six thirty is fine."

Maria popped her head in at that moment and smiled. "Aaron, it's good to see you in here. Finn mentioned starting you with the pups. It's one of the better ideas he's had in a while. I hope it wasn't too soon, though. How are you doing?"

"Well, I'm alive," he admitted. "I held one of the huskies. It was soft." *It was soft? What am I, three again?* Inwardly, he cringed.

"They are little furballs. They'll get adopted quickly. They get put up next week on Monday. I wouldn't be surprised if they get adopted in pairs, actually. Maybe I'll cut the adoption fee…"

Aaron glanced at Finn as he went back to work and reached over to hand him a clean bottle of water, standing back from the cage in case one tried to escape.

"I'm very pleased with your progress, Aaron. And proud of you. I know it must be hard, but you've made tremendous progress in your first two days. That's a huge step. You're really pushing yourself."

"I'm not ready—"

"I know you're not ready for more. That's okay." Maria smiled. "Start with the puppies and then we can build you up. Small dogs to large. You take all the time you need. We don't want to lose you as a volunteer! You've been a great help already."

Once again Aaron's face flushed from embarrassment, but also from pride at having made such an impression, despite having been late the first day. *I just hope I don't screw things up.*

CHAPTER FOUR

The clock read six thirty when Aaron pulled up to Gracie's Restaurant. He hadn't wanted to be too early or too late for this meeting. Finn stood apart from the small crowd gathered, leaning against the hood of his beat-up car. Parts of the car were different shades of blue, with the exception of one dull gray panel. A few minor dents and dings graced the rear right fender of the car, and on the hood a circle of paint had peeled away. Aaron instantly understood what Finn had meant by rough condition.

Finn saw him as he locked his car and grinned.

"Cool, just in time. We're lucky—the major crowd left a few minutes ago, so we'll get a booth."

Aaron nodded and followed him in. A waitress at the door greeted the boys and brought them to a booth in the rear of the restaurant. She set down the menus without much fanfare and disappeared as they took their seats.

"How did the rest of work go? Did you stay with the dogs?"

"No, I went back to work with the cats. They needed to be fed."

"Oh, well that's cool. Did you get to work with Molly?"

"Yeah."

Finn picked up his menu. "She's cool. She's been working there forever. Just a few hours on Saturday. She does a lot of fostering for cats, though. Has a huge house with one room built just for them. It has all these posts for them to climb on. It's kind of like a kitty amusement park."

"She sort of reminds me of my grandmother," Aaron admitted, and Finn laughed.

"She reminds everybody of their grandmother. She has that sweet old lady vibe to her, but her jokes can be downright dirty sometimes."

Aaron followed Finn's lead and picked up his menu. He already knew what he wanted, though. Ever since Finn had mentioned a burger at the shelter, his mouth had been watering for one.

"Enough shoptalk. What's your life like outside the shelter? I don't know much, just that you go to Central High. Our rival." He winked. "And I know you have a cat named Midnight. That's about it."

"What do you want to know? There isn't much to tell, honestly," Aaron lied.

"Do you play any sports? Siblings? Wait, I'm going to say no on the siblings because you would have mentioned one by now."

"Correct."

"I'm good. Okay, so sports?" Finn asked.

"None."

"Really?"

Aaron shrugged. "I'm not the most athletic guy, I guess. Some of my friends play on the baseball team. I just never got into sports. I played on a league when I was a kid because my dad wanted me to, but I didn't care for it. What about you?"

"No time, are you kidding?"

"Kind of figured that, but do you like any sports?"

Finn grabbed a straw from the cup at the edge of the table and tapped the end on the flat surface, breaking the paper wrapper around the straw and bunching it toward the bottom. He tried to blow the wrapper off the end but failed and finally just pulled it off. "I like swimming, but not competitively. I just like to float around during the summer."

"Yeah, me, too."

"Okay, so no siblings and no sports, one cat. What do your parents do?"

"My mom is a nurse and my dad is a real estate agent."

"That's cool. Are they home at the same time or does your mom work a night shift or something?"

"My parents got divorced three years ago. Mom works during the day most of the time so we can hang out at night. She likes sitting down together for dinner. Dad has his own house in Burlington."

Finn's face fell. "Oh, dude. I'm sorry. I had no idea. That sucks."

Aaron shrugged. "It is what it is. It's not that bad, actually. I miss my dad being home, but I talk to him a lot. I see him on the weekends when he's not too busy and stay at his house sometimes. He's only the next town over so it's okay. And now that I can drive, I can visit more if he can't come out to get me."

"Did your parents fight a lot before they got divorced?"

"Not really in front of me. I could tell things weren't good because they didn't talk as much as they used to, and one of them always seemed to be out of the house, but it wasn't bad. They talk to each other now all right. At least they do when I'm around. Dad called last night and Mom talked to him on the phone for a bit."

"Some people just make better friends, I guess," Finn said.

Their conversation stopped as the waitress returned to take their order. They both ordered Cokes and burgers with fries, but Finn added avocado to his.

"I love it," he said after he caught Aaron staring at him. "I could eat it on everything."

Aaron made a face. "Not me. It's gross. It has the weirdest texture."

"More for me then," Finn teased. "Anyway, you're lucky your parents get along, even if they are divorced. My house is like a battle zone." He lowered his voice and glanced around before leaning in to Aaron. "To be honest, sometimes I wish my parents would get a divorce."

"Why would you want that?" Aaron stared at him in surprise. Everyone he knew with a broken family wished it had never happened and wanted life back to what it had been in their childhood.

Finn shrugged and tapped the straw against the table. "Like I said, battle zone. I don't have any siblings, so my parents use me to get at each other. If Dad's mad at Mom, he complains to me about what a horrible, lazy person she is. When Mom's mad at Dad, she threatens to divorce him and tells me how I better not turn into a jerk like him." He sighed. "I don't know why they don't just get it over with. They've both threatened to serve each other with papers for years now."

Aaron didn't know what to say. Even his face was frozen as he stared at his new friend. Finn looked miserable as he sat there, still tapping the end of his straw against the wood. It crumpled and Finn grabbed another one, tearing the paper wrapper from it. The waitress arrived with their Cokes and set them down, momentarily freeing Aaron from his obligation to speak. He took the opportunity to take a long sip of his drink as he searched for the right words to say.

"It's no wonder you work so much, then. You're saving up for college, sure, but it also gets you out of the house," he finally managed.

Finn nodded. "Pretty much, yeah. It helps. When I'm working, I'm surrounded by books, and they don't talk. Neither do the animals. Plus the animals are a real stress relief. Walking the dogs is great, it really is. It gets me out of my head when I focus on something else. The dogs don't care what kind of day you've had or what you've had to put up with. They just want some love and affection. It's unconditional love of the best kind." Finn paused and then laughed awkwardly. "That probably sounds really cheesy. Sorry."

Aaron talked with him more about their families until dinner arrived, and then they took a few minutes to eat in silence. *Should I just come out and tell him I'm gay?* He took a large bite from his burger. He glanced up at Finn as he grabbed the ketchup, shook it, and nearly splattered it over both of them as the bottle erupted on his plate.

A piece of his burger flew out of his mouth as he laughed and choked. Finn stared down in disgust at the red stain on his shirt. "Man, I just washed this shirt! You know, this happens every time I eat," he complained, causing Aaron to laugh even harder.

"I used to be the same way when I was a kid. Every time I ate ice cream, it ended up all over my face! My parents used to joke that if I ever went on a date, they'd be behind him holding up a napkin to remind me—" Aaron cut himself off as he realized his slip and immediately busied himself by noisily slurping his drink.

Finn cursed as he wiped his shirt with the napkin, moistened with the condensation on his glass.

Aaron continued to eat his burger and fries, his face warmed as he waited for a reaction from Finn. When a minute had passed, he wondered if Finn had even heard him. He certainly seemed busy wiping the red glob off his shirt. Could it be possible Finn hadn't caught it?

As one minute passed into two, sweat built up along his hairline just like before. He was tired of sweating. Before it could make its presence known and trickle down the side of his face, he reached up and brushed it away discreetly as if he was brushing his hair out of his eyes.

"What did you say before? Sorry, I got distracted."

Aaron swallowed the bite of his burger. "Just that I made a mess of myself as a kid eating ice cream, so I feel your pain."

"Yeah, but what did you say about your parents? It sounded funny. I don't know them, but I could picture parents doing that to embarrass the hell out of their kid."

"It happened before the divorce. They still mention it sometimes. Any time I eat ice cream, actually. It kind of gets old, you know?"

Finn nodded. "I can imagine." He took a bite of his burger, set it down as he chewed thoughtfully, and rested his chin on his hands as he gazed at Aaron. The look he gave Aaron made him fidget in his seat as if he was under the knife, about to be dissected. "You said something else."

Dammit. He heard what I said.

"No, just that."

"Are you sure?"

"Positive."

Finn frowned. "I swear, I thought I heard you say something else."

"What did I supposedly say?" Aaron asked, pushing some fries around his plate. *Guilty conscience? Me? Never.* He mentally cursed himself for not being able to hide his emotions well. He blamed his fire-red hair and pale skin.

"I could have sworn—not that it matters—that you said *him.* Like your parents would sit behind *him* as in your date, *him.*"

"Not that it matters, you said."

"Right," Finn agreed. "It wouldn't matter one way or the other. Him, her." He waved a hand vaguely. "Who am I to judge? Look at my family."

Aaron relaxed immediately and smiled across the table at Finn, who returned it with one of his own.

"So, it's true?"

"That I'm gay? Yes."

"I thought so."

"You did? Why?"

"It's no problem, Aaron. Not at all."

"Any reason you're so...okay with it?" *Like, maybe you're gay, too, and I have a chance with you?*

"Like I said, look at my family. I see nothing wrong with it. You are who you are. And as far as I'm concerned, love is love. I'd much rather see that than war, you know? Two guys who love each other and are happy with life are worse than a senseless war where thousands of soldiers are killed because of their leader's beliefs? I don't see it." Finn shrugged. "Having a family like mine...it makes you look at things differently."

Aaron felt foolish for being nervous about telling Finn. "Did you know there used to be this army made up entirely of gay men? They're called the Sacred Band of Thebes," Aaron babbled and nearly gushed as he told him about it.

"I didn't know that," Finn said as he scooped up a fry. "That's pretty neat. And just think, a few years ago our own military banned gays and lesbians from serving openly." He snorted. "Looks like government should read the history books!"

The two of them laughed and Aaron felt the weight of the world lift off his shoulders. Having a friend like Finn would be great for him. He could be himself and not worry about what he talked about, like with everyone else. *And if Finn does turn out to be gay...*He stopped himself. No way could he be that lucky. "I've done a lot of research. It's a subject that fascinates me. Maybe it's just because *I* am. I don't know. But there's more out there. So much of it doesn't make it into the history books."

"There is a lot that doesn't make it," Finn agreed. "History books are biased. Plus there's so much history, they have to cut some stuff out. I don't agree with all of what they cut, but I will admit they have to draw the line somewhere. Then again, some of the junk they keep in there is so pointless. I think more people would be interested in history if they knew about the other side of it, like what you said."

Aaron agreed with him and they finished off their burgers. "There are other gay theories and stuff about some Egyptian pharaohs, and then there's Hadrian and Antinous."

"I think it's cool you know so much. Ever think about being a teacher?"

"A teacher of what?" Aaron made a face. "Gay history? Maybe a college course, but even then, is there even a college that would offer that?"

"You never know. You could always slip the information into high school history courses. I'm sure it would keep the students awake."

"And get me fired. No, I don't really know what I want to do yet. I've got some time before college. You're lucky you already know. I kind of envy that."

Finn threw a fry at him, hitting Aaron square in the chest. It left behind a small grease stain. "Hey, like you said, you've got time. You'll figure everything out. So, are you dating anyone?"

"Nope," Aaron said, holding his breath.

"Have you ever?"

"Negative."

"Don't tell me you don't know anyone else who's gay," Finn said, sounding skeptical.

"Sure I do," Aaron replied with a frown. "My school is huge. There's a Gay Straight Alliance there. But no one interests me. Besides, it's not like the GSA is for hooking up. It's to talk about issues and history, making changes in the world." He paused. "So, do you, uh, have a girlfriend?"

Finn laughed. "Are you kidding? Of course not. I don't have time, remember? I did have a girlfriend. But she wasn't happy that my schedule was so tight, so she broke it off. I got over it, though. It would've been nice, but I know what I need to focus on right now."

"You really are a unique guy, Finn," Aaron said, masking his disappointment though his shoulders did slump. *Of course he's not gay. That would be too perfect.*

Finn didn't seem to notice. "I try."

CHAPTER FIVE

Aaron wasn't scheduled to volunteer on Sunday. Part of him wanted to go in just to play with the cats, but he needed to get homework done, too. Compared to Finn, he felt inferior. He had so much free time compared to his friend, and yet his grades weren't as high as they could be.

His mother found him at noon, lounging on his bed with his copy of *The Grapes of Wrath* and papers from class spread around him.

"Well, isn't this a pleasant surprise," she exclaimed as she knocked on his door frame. "You're willingly doing your English homework? What brought that about?"

"My grades are pathetic compared to Finn's, and he works *and* volunteers at the shelter."

"Two days and this kid has already become my new favorite person. When is he coming over for dinner?"

Aaron rolled his eyes. "Mom, please."

"No, really. I'm glad you've made a new friend, Aaron. Especially one who's going to be such a good influence on you."

"Mom." His face heated with embarrassment and he ducked his head into the book. "Did you come up here for something?"

She frowned. "Actually, yes. Tyler and Caleb stopped by last night. I forgot to tell you."

He sat up straighter in his bed. "Really? What did they want?"

"They said they were stopping by to see if you wanted to hang out, but I told them you were out. I didn't tell them where, though. I thought that might not be any of their business. I haven't seen them around much." She studied his expression. "They aren't giving you trouble, are they?"

With a sigh, Aaron shrugged and put the book down. His mother looked concerned. "Not trouble, no. But we've kind of lost touch, so I'm surprised they stopped by."

"Your father mentioned something about that. Why didn't you tell me?"

"It's not that big of a deal, Mom. People grow apart all the time. They do their thing, I do mine." When she didn't move from the doorway, Aaron gave her a reassuring smile. "Dad just asked how they were doing, that's all. And I'm fine, really. It's not like I'm a social pariah. I talk to people at school."

"Okay. If you say so. I trust your judgment." She turned to leave and then hesitated. "I really do want you to invite Finn for dinner the next time you see him."

"Okay, Mom. Whatever you say."

When she finally left, Aaron picked up his cell and sent a quick text to Finn, inviting him to dinner, per his mother, at his convenience. The response came back almost instantly and made him smile: *LOL! Tell your mother I would be honored to partake in a meal. I have Thursday night free, if that's good for her.*

Aaron responded that it was good and put his book away. He'd been reading for an hour and deserved a break before his brain melted out of his ears. He smoothed Midnight's fur as he passed him and proceeded downstairs, where his mother was sitting on the couch watching a show she had recorded on the DVR.

"Finn said Thursday is good if it's good for you."

"Thursday is fine. I'll make sure to take out a pot roast. Oh! Or is he vegetarian?"

"We had a burger last night at Gracie's, so I'm gonna go with no. But you don't have to go through all the trouble, Mom. Anything would be fine. I can make pasta before you come home. It will be quick, easy, and cheap."

"Well look at you, aren't you suddenly the thrifty one." She smiled. "No, I'll make a pot roast. I can put it in the Crock-Pot before I go to work in the morning, and by the time we're ready to eat, it'll be finished. It will give us leftovers, too. Do you think we should do dessert?"

"Mom, no. This isn't supposed to be some huge deal. No dessert."

"Fine, fine. Whatever you say. You run the show." She sounded serious, but she said it with the smile still on her face.

Despite the rift in his friendship with Caleb and Tyler, Aaron did want to see what they were up to, so he grabbed his phone from where it was charging. "I'll be back in a bit. Just going out for a walk." If she heard him she didn't say anything, so he strolled out the front door and shut it behind him.

The air was warm and he enjoyed the walk down the block. Tyler lived a few streets over, but Caleb was just around the corner. There had been many days when the three of them rode their bikes back and forth between the houses in all kinds of weather. It was a shame things had shifted, but if they had stopped by...maybe there was a chance they were coming around. *Stranger things have happened.*

Caleb's front door was wide open, and Aaron could hear his dog barking from the back of the house. He breathed a sigh of relief as he knocked on the door, knowing the hyperactive boxer would not come charging at the door to get to him.

The door opened and Caleb's mother smiled warmly at him. "Aaron, it's been a while since I've seen you. Come on in."

"Thanks, Mrs. Hendricks. Is Caleb around?"

"Yes, he's up in his room. Go on up."

"Sure," he said, waving as he took the stairs two at a time.

Caleb's bedroom was the last one in the hallway on the left and looked over the backyard. The door was partially cracked open with band posters covering the outside of it. He knocked before pushing it in.

"Mom! I told you to—Oh. Hey, Aaron. I didn't know you were coming over." Caleb sat up quickly on his bed and shoved a magazine down the side against the wall and the mattress. Aaron bit back a laugh.

"You stopped by my house last night. I figured I'd see what you were up to. And really, your door was open, man. You want to hide that stuff from your mom at least shut the door and give yourself more time to hide the evidence."

Caleb narrowed his eyes. "What would you know about it?"

Aaron rolled his. "Come on, it's obvious. But whatever. Just stopping by to see what you were doing. Mom said you wanted to hang out."

His friend shrugged and swung his feet off the side of the bed. "Tyler and I were bored and in the area. We didn't have anything in mind. Just thought we'd say hello. Didn't think you'd really be home anyway."

"Why wouldn't I be home?"

Caleb shrugged again and pushed himself off the bed before crossing his arms. "Don't know. You're weird now. Who knows what you're up to these days."

The sigh slipped past Aaron's lips before he could stop it from escaping. "What is that supposed to mean? I'm weird now? I'm the same person, Caleb. You didn't have a problem with me last year."

"Yeah, that was before you were gay."

Throwing up his hands in exasperation, he backed to the doorway and leaned against it. "I've always been gay! It didn't happen overnight, you know."

"Whatever. You were straight to us one day, gay the next. How else are we supposed to take it? It's weird, man."

"We? You mean you and Tyler?"

"Yeah. Of course."

Aaron had been through this before. How could he keep explaining himself to them? It was like they didn't get it, and maybe they didn't understand. But it was hard for him, too. "Well, how am I supposed to take my best friends changing on *me*? I didn't change, did I? Did I start to talk differently?"

"No," Caleb admitted.

"Do I act differently?"

"Not really, no."

"Do I talk about it?"

Caleb frowned. "No?"

"And I know for a fact that I have never mentioned liking any guy to you or interrupted you two when you're talking about girls."

"Okay, fine, I guess I get your point. But…I don't know. I'm just not comfortable with it. Tyler's not either."

"You two never said anything to me about being uncomfortable. We could have talked about this before now, you know. Did you think I didn't notice you two backing off? We were good friends, Caleb. The three of us."

"Yeah, I know…" Caleb had the grace to look at the ground and awkwardly shoved his hands in his pockets.

"When that dog attacked me, you guys were cool with it. You put your own dogs outside so I can—could—hang out with you two."

"That's different. The thing with the dog wasn't your fault. I mean, you didn't choose that."

"I didn't choose that? I didn't choose to be gay! It's who I am, Caleb. Do you really think I woke up one morning and decided, hey, I want my friends to ostracize me? That sounds like fun. No! I'm fine with who I am, but I didn't choose this."

Caleb shifted from one foot to the other. "Maybe you should go, Aaron. It's been cool and all, but we're just different people now."

Aaron snorted. "I'm not different. You're the one who is. You and Tyler both." Before Caleb could respond, Aaron turned and marched down the steps. Caleb's mother was in the kitchen, and he gave her a short good-bye before letting himself out the front door.

If that was how Caleb was going to react, he wasn't going to bother with Tyler. He would just act the same way. At least Aaron had gotten an answer, and he could officially move on and forget about them.

His insides twisted uncomfortably. Losing them did bother him because he had been friends with them for so long, but he would cut his losses. He didn't want to be friends with people who couldn't accept him for who he was. He'd just met Finn and he'd been a better friend to him in two days than the other two had been in the last year. Strange how things happened.

CHAPTER SIX

Finn had mentioned working at the local bookstore, Between the Pages, on Monday, and Aaron had gotten his hours the night before. After school, he drove downtown to the small, independently owned bookstore. Usually he went to the mall, to the larger chain bookstore. They always had more of a selection to browse, but if Finn worked here, he'd try to support this one now.

When he entered the store, he was almost overpowered by the scent of fresh coffee. A chime on the door jingled pleasantly as it shut behind him, and a girl behind the counter smiled and greeted him. He smiled back at her before he made his way into the store.

It was far from large, but it wasn't as small as he had thought, either. Bookshelves lined all the walls except for the left rear corner. In this back section, a small counter was set up with chalkboards on the wall. One employee stood behind the counter while a customer sat on a barstool in front of it, sipping from a white mug.

There were tables placed around the store with books displayed on them. Comfortable-looking, worn chairs were positioned in convenient locations, and one of them was occupied. He made his way deeper into the store, peering around the standing shelves to find Finn.

He found him in the back alcove, shelving books and shifting them around. Aaron watched him for a moment, listening as he repeated the alphabet back to himself, half singing it.

"E, F, G, H, I...I...there."

Aaron cleared his throat. "Hey, Finn. Glad to see you remember your ABCs."

Finn jumped a little and turned, grinning. "I didn't even hear you. I should pay more attention. What if you were a customer looking for help?"

"Who's to say I'm *not* a customer looking for help?"

"True," he acknowledged. "So, what can I help you find?"

"Nothing," Aaron said with a sheepish grin. "Just coming to visit you."

"Cool. It's pretty quiet today, so I can talk for a bit and we shouldn't be interrupted. Do you want to get a cup of coffee and hang out while I shelve these books?"

"Maybe later." Aaron found an empty chair nearby and sank into it. "So, any good new books lately?"

Finn laughed and shrugged. "Well, what genre are you looking for? There are always new books coming out. Every week there's something for everyone. Though, let me guess, you'd be interested in history."

"Or any LGBT fiction."

"We might have a few. I would have to check—I don't know any titles offhand. And if we do have anything, you've probably already read it. The larger chain stores get a better selection than we do, but the owner's pretty good. She knows what her customers like and orders accordingly."

"To be honest, I don't usually go to small stores like this."

"That's a shame," Finn said. He sighed. "But most people don't. You can find some really good things here. And besides, we can always order books if we don't have what you want. I like smaller stores better because you seem to know the staff more, you know? We have a lot of faithful customers who come in every day, even if it's just to get a cup of coffee. It's pretty cool."

"Well, maybe you can convince me to shop here more."

"Hopefully, I can," he said with a wink.

Is he flirting with me? I thought he said he had a girlfriend before. Maybe he's bisexual? Aaron's eyes narrowed, his lips pursing as he tried to figure out what Finn meant.

Finn placed the last book on the shelf and turned to his cart, grabbed another handful, and moved to another section of the wall. "Did school suck as much as you thought it might today?"

Aaron gave a halfhearted shrug and slumped farther into the seat. "It wasn't as bad as I thought. I wondered how Caleb and Tyler would react when they saw me, but I didn't run into them like usual. Maybe I passed them and didn't notice."

"Or maybe they avoided you. But…they wouldn't *do* anything to you, would they?" Finn pulled back, looking startled by the thought.

Aaron smiled. "Nothing like that. Neither has it in him. But we've been friends for so long, and those friendships are definitely over. I don't think anything could repair them at this point."

Finn nodded sympathetically. "I'm sorry they're being such assholes about it. There's not much I can say, but they're not worth it if they're going to let this bother them."

"I know realistically you're right. It still hurts, though."

"Of course it does. But it'll get better. Besides, you can hang out with me now, and I know for a fact I'm cooler," he said with a grin. "Maybe you can get to know some of my friends. Not that I see them much, either, with all my free time."

Aaron picked up the book on the table next to him and flipped through it. "Yeah, maybe."

Their conversation lapsed as Finn went back to work and Aaron found himself becoming absorbed in the mystery novel he had happened to grab at random. The silence between them wasn't awkward. In fact, it was comfortable. Aaron felt as if he was in a bubble of comfort. The pages were crisp beneath his fingers, the scent of coffee wafted under his nose, and every so often he could hear the front door chime ring quietly through the air. He was warm but not overly so, and his eyelids drooped as the words began to blur across the page.

"Hey, don't fall asleep," Finn warned jokingly as he placed a hand on his shoulder. Aaron did not expect the touch and nearly jumped out of his skin.

"How long have I been here?"

"Not long, really. Only about forty-five minutes. You didn't fall asleep or anything, but you looked like you were about to."

"This place is comfortable. It's so relaxing compared to the place I usually go to. Quieter. Like a library."

"Told you."

Aaron picked up the book he had been reading. "I should probably head home before I really fall asleep. This book is pretty good. I think I'm going to get it."

"It's been a decent seller, but I haven't read it myself. Let me know how it is."

"Sure. I'll see you on Thursday for dinner, right?"

Finn grinned. "Wouldn't miss it."

Aaron gathered the book he wanted, waved to Finn, and headed over to the coffee counter. He ordered a mocha to go, then went up front to where the girl had greeted him and paid for the book. She babbled to him the whole time, but he didn't really pay attention to her words. After thanking her, he headed out the door and climbed into his car.

The sun dipped below the horizon as he made his way home. Dinner would be ready soon, and he still had some homework left to do. His mother's car wasn't in the driveway when he pulled in, and he wondered if she was working a late shift. Normally she texted when she was running late, but a check on his phone revealed nothing.

Taking out his keys, Aaron opened the front door as his mother's car pulled into the driveway. He flipped on the lights inside to chase back the shadows and reached down to scoop up Midnight. "Hey, kitty." The old cat purred and butted his head against his chin as he held him close.

"Sorry. I meant to beat you home. I thought you would be gone a little longer," his mother said as she climbed out of the car. She held bags in her hand and brought them straight to the kitchen as Aaron shut the door behind her and set Midnight on the ground. The cat trotted after her, turning his head as if to tell Aaron to follow.

"Did you pick up dinner?"

"Yes, I figured we'd go with something different today. I wasn't much in the mood for cooking."

Aaron set his coffee and bag on the counter. "Does that mean we're low on edible food?"

His mother laughed and he smiled at the sound. He remembered when she had been so upset by the divorce it was hard to make her smile, let alone laugh. It came much more freely now.

"Yes, it means the cupboard is almost bare. Old Mother Hubbard will have to go shopping after we eat. How was your visit with Finn?"

"It was okay. The bookstore he works at is cool. He's still excited to come over on Thursday." He pulled out containers of Chinese food and set them on the counter. His mother pulled out forks and bowls and they popped open each of the cartons and took what they wanted out of each small box. "I told him what happened with Caleb and Tyler. He repeated what you said."

"I like this Finn. I look forward to meeting him."

"You'll like him. But remember what I said—don't ask him about his family, okay? It really bothers him having his parents fight all the time. I can't even imagine…"

"It's a harsh reality. Divorces don't always end well. You're lucky in that respect. Your father and I just didn't see eye to eye anymore, and we decided it was best to part ways before things got ugly. We didn't want to resent each other and make it harder for you than it needed to be. Some parents don't understand that by staying together sometimes they're making matters worse."

"But he said they're not getting divorced, just threatening to do it. How could they put him through that?"

His mother shrugged as she popped a piece of teriyaki chicken into her mouth. "I don't know. I don't understand it myself."

CHAPTER SEVEN

The doorbell rang Thursday afternoon and Aaron ran to get the door. "I've got it," he called to his mother as she dropped a pot in the kitchen and swore. "You okay?"

"I'm fine. Just let him in."

Aaron opened the door to find Finn's back to him as he looked around the neighborhood. "Hey."

Finn turned, not even pretending to be surprised, and waved a hand briefly. "Hey. Thanks for having me over."

"It's nothing. Come on," he said as he motioned for Finn to move inside.

His friend seemed to be taking everything in as he glanced down at Aaron's bare feet and toed off his shoes. "Nice neighborhood," he finally said, and Aaron cocked his head to one side. His friend was acting…different. If he had to put a name to it, maybe a bit tense or nervous.

What would he have to be nervous for?

"Mom, Finn is here," he called into the kitchen. His mother's smiling face peered around the corner. "Nice to meet you. I've heard so much about you."

"Likewise, ma'am," Finn said, all sincere and polite.

"Dinner will be ready in a minute."

"Come on," Aaron said, "I'll show you around."

Leading Finn upstairs, he gave him a quick tour of the house, stopping at his room. Finn peered inside, looked around, and then slipped back to the stairs without saying a word.

"Your house is pretty neat," he said after they had gone downstairs and taken seats in the dining room.

"It is cool, I guess."

"No, neat like clean. Everything has its place."

"That's Mom."

As if she heard Aaron, his mother came out with the pot roast in a large dish. "Hope you boys are hungry."

"Starving," Finn said. He stared at the dish as she set it on the table and a small frown pulled at his lips.

Aaron remained silent and watched as his mother attempted to serve them, but Finn interrupted and offered to do it. She smiled brightly and gestured, then took her seat. The frown vanished from Finn's face, but Aaron knew what he saw. He just didn't know why.

Aaron strode into the shelter after school on Friday with a smile on his face. Dinner the night before with Finn and his mother had been great. It was nice to have a friend hang out without the other boy acting as if Aaron would jump him at any moment. His mother was relaxed, too, and took to Finn in a way she'd never taken to any of his other friends. Finn was just that way: charming, sweet, smart, and irresistible. After he'd left, Aaron had a fleeting moment wishing a relationship with Finn was a possibility.

There was that odd moment when the food came out that, after a night spent analyzing it, had Aaron unsure of what he'd seen or why. Finn had seemed...confused. By what, Aaron wasn't sure, and he didn't know how to bring it up. What if it had been a misunderstanding?

Smiling at Sandra as he passed through the lobby, he went to the staff room to see what he was scheduled for that day. What sat in the middle of the floor surprised him, and he threw himself backward until he hit the wall on the opposite side of the hallway.

Attached to a leash that Maria held on to firmly was a large, brown dog. The wide face and broad forehead screamed pit bull. Aaron's heart slammed to a stop in his chest before it began to beat double time. The dog turned to look at him with large, blank eyes, and Aaron immediately saw the scars running alongside the face.

"We can't put him in quarantine with the sick dogs if he's not sick," Maria was saying as she held on to the leash in her hand. "And we can't have him share one of the larger kennels. I don't know what he'll do to the other dogs. We don't know what his temperament is."

"Is it safe to keep him?" Amy asked, standing away from the dog but leaning in to examine him. "He looks like he's in bad shape."

"Animal control assured me he wasn't a problem. They found him in an abandoned lot after they received a call. He was tied to a post in the center. They suspect the lot's been used by a dog-fighting ring. No other dogs were found at the site except this one. Poor thing, he's so beaten up."

"Why did they bring him here?" Finn asked from the other side of the room. His arms were crossed over his chest as he leaned against the counter.

"No one else has room for him."

Finn snorted. "More like they didn't want him."

Maria sighed. "Finn, please."

"Sorry."

"Maria, we don't have the facilities to care for a dog like this. Or the manpower."

Maria sighed and leaned down to gingerly pat the dog's head. He responded by wagging his tail weakly. "They were going to just put him down. We were his last chance. I don't know, when I saw how calm he was, I couldn't let them. There's potential here."

"Are they going to investigate?" Finn asked.

"They said they would, but Officer Hardy doesn't think it's likely they'll find who did this. He has no microchip, and no one is coming forward with information about who left him behind," Maria said.

"He's scarred. People aren't going to want to adopt a pit bull looking like that. They'll think he's trouble," Amy said. Aaron's movement away from the wall caught her eye and she turned to him, her face turning red. "Oh my gosh, Aaron! We didn't see you come in."

"W-what is that?" Aaron asked, still standing in the hallway but using the door frame as a shield. His legs trembled with the urge to leave.

Finn took a step closer to him, casually putting himself between Aaron and the dog. "A pit bull animal control just brought in."

"He doesn't look like any pit bull I've seen."

"He's been attacked. We think the owners used him as a bait dog to train other dogs to fight."

"Then he's dangerous," Aaron stated.

Maria shook her head. "No. Not all abused dogs end up aggressive, and he certainly doesn't seem to be from what I've seen so far. Other dogs who have been attacked or trained to attack act with aggression from the start. The officer said when he was rescued, he just sat and wagged his tail, despite his extensive injuries. Since he's been here, he's been nothing but a good boy."

Aaron's heart pounded in his chest and he took another step backward. Scars covered a large portion of the dog's body, and some of them were clearly new, with angry red scabs that had barely begun to heal. On his face was a scar almost identical to the one on Aaron's face that ran from his eye to his lip. He could feel what pain the dog must have been through, having gone through it himself, but that deeply rooted fear still clutched him, and he couldn't face this pit bull, no matter how good and gentle he'd been so far.

"I...I'm just going to check on the cats," he said, bolting from the doorway.

When Finn found him, Aaron was sitting on the floor in the far corner of the hallway with his back pressed against the wall. He'd gathered a group of the free-roaming cats around him like a shield and played with them with a piece of string he'd found. As he waved it back and forth in front of the group, the cats watched, turning their heads in unison, and then pounced on it and each other in their struggle to be the one to win the prize.

"Are you okay?" Finn asked as he slid down the wall and sat next to him. He was close, but not enough to touch.

"I'm definitely not ready to work with the dogs," Aaron stated, not bothering to look at Finn.

"Why do you say that? You did great with the puppies last week. Don't fall back in your progress."

"It was too soon, I think."

"No, it wasn't. What's wrong, Aaron? Is it the pit bull?"

Aaron stared at the string and held it up just out of reach of the cats and watched as they jumped and twisted in the air trying to get it. "It's a dog. All dogs are the same to me. Doesn't matter what breed they are."

Finn eyed him, turning a bit to get a better view of his face. Aaron tilted his head down and let his hair cover the scars. He wished Finn would've sat on the other side of him, away from the ugly reminder.

"It's the way he looks, isn't it?"

"Who am I to judge someone else's scars?"

"Not all dogs are bad. And yeah, he might look a bit scary, but inside he's just as scared as you are. I'm sure of it."

"How can you be so sure he's a good dog? You heard what they said about how he was found. How he got those scars. He could turn on people or dogs anytime."

"He's had a hard life. You can't hold that against him. We can help him."

"You can, maybe. Count me out."

"I don't think that dog would hurt a fly. He responded so well to everyone and just look at him. Think of the abuse he's suffered."

"They said he's a fighting dog."

"I bet he refused to fight and that's why he was used as a bait dog."

"What's that?" Aaron asked, against his better judgment.

"A bait dog, from what I understand, is a dog who won't fight, so it's used to train other dogs to fight, or to show off that another dog won't back off in the ring. Some dogs, no matter what situation they're in or who their owner is, just refuse to fight."

Even though Aaron didn't like dogs, the thought of someone doing that to any animal sickened him. He turned to look at Finn. "But what makes you so sure that dog won't turn on you and snap?"

Finn shrugged and leaned against the wall. "*Any* dog could turn on you and snap. You witnessed that firsthand. But sometimes you have to give a little trust to get it. If you show an animal you're afraid, it will react to that fear. Animals can smell it. But they can be afraid, too. Some scared dogs cower and try to hide, others show aggression, but it stems from the same thing—fear." He paused for a few minutes, and the two sat in silence as the cats played or slept around them. "The scars are frightening, but that's it."

"One of his scars…it looks like mine."

"I noticed that, too. You've both been attacked by a dog. Or multiple dogs, in his case. And…I think in some ways you share the same issues regarding people."

"What issues are those?"

"People look at each of you and see something they don't like."

Aaron cringed and drew back from Finn, but his friend grabbed his arm and turned him so their eyes met.

"I'm not saying you're frightening, Aaron. I hardly notice the scars now that I know you. But I'm talking about what you told me about Caleb and Tyler."

"What do they have to do with anything?"

"They looked at you and didn't see the real you, did they? They saw *one* aspect of you. They didn't take the time to put all the pieces together to see that you're a cool guy. They just wanted to see that you were gay, and they didn't like that, so automatically you were… someone else in their eyes."

After a moment, Aaron grudgingly nodded. What Finn said made sense.

"People are going to look at that dog the same way you just did and see one aspect of him—his scars. They'll jump to conclusions because that's what people do. He's a pit bull, so he's vicious, and because he has scars, he must be even worse than the others. He must be a fighter. They won't look at the wagging tail or the tongue lolling out of his mouth ready to greet them in friendship."

Even though the fear was still there, Aaron did understand the reaction the dog would face once Finn pointed it out to him. In fact, he felt ashamed of himself for thinking that way. It was a dog, yes, but just like him, the dog was a victim of circumstance. Aaron had reacted exactly as Finn predicted others would.

"Is he really friendly?"

Finn nodded. "Yes. He shies away from loud people, but if you let him approach you he warms up quickly."

"Kind of like I shy away from dogs?"

Finn laughed. "No offense, but you don't shy away from them. You bolt in the opposite direction." Aaron joined in the laughter despite the heat creeping up his neck.

"I guess you're right."

"Do you think…?" Finn started and then trailed off as his eyes glazed over. Aaron leaned forward to look at him and tilted his head to the side.

"Do I think what?"

"I had a thought. It might sound crazy, but hear me out, okay?" When Aaron nodded he continued. "You have a lot in common with this dog. You're both afraid of other dogs. Some people have hurt you—and Caleb and Tyler have, whether you say they have or not, because they abused your friendship—and you both carry the physical and emotional scars from your ordeals. What if we ask Maria if you can work with the dog? Either she will be there or me and another trained handler, so you'll be safe. Since you share so many things with him, maybe it would be easier to overcome your fears."

Aaron opened his mouth to reject the idea immediately, but he pushed the voice back. He *had* made a little progress with his fear. He had been in a room filled with dogs in cages, and he had even held a puppy.

Did he want to do this?

Yes. It made the most sense.

But *could* he do this?

That's the real question, isn't it?

"Are you sure you're not training to become a psychologist?"

Finn chuckled. "Yeah, I'm sure."

"Do you really think it's a good idea?"

"I think it's the best idea for you right now. Other dogs can be hyper and might be tempted to jump all over you. Given the condition of the new guy and his past, it's unlikely he's going to behave that way. And we'll be there for you."

"Okay," Aaron said after a moment. "I'll talk to Maria about it. Well, we will, if you don't mind coming with me. I think you make the whole thing sound better."

The two of them got off the floor, sending a flurry of cats running in all directions. Aaron followed Finn out of the room and made sure no cats escaped behind him as he shut the door securely. Maria was still in the employees' room with the dog. He lay on the floor at her feet, head between his paws, as she held on to his leash. Amy looked up when they entered and gave them a small smile.

Aaron stepped into the room and eased against the wall. He stood close to the door in case the fear overwhelmed him, but he moved farther into the room than he had been before.

"Maria, we were hoping we could talk to you about something," Finn announced.

"Who exactly is *we*?"

"Aaron and I."

"Sure, but later? I'm kind of in the middle of something."

"If that something is the pit bull, then that's what we wanted to talk to you about."

Maria raised an eyebrow and studied the two boys, her gaze lingering, it seemed, on Aaron. "Go ahead."

"Well I—we—were thinking maybe it would be a good idea for Aaron to work with this dog," Finn said before launching into his litany of reasons for the idea and how it would benefit both human and animal alike. "Of course, we would wait until he passes the SAFER test, and if he doesn't, then…well, obviously it's out of the question."

Maria looked thoughtful, if a bit skeptical. Aaron didn't blame her—he felt the same way. Her lips shifted down in a thoughtful frown and she kept glancing at the canine at her feet. He kept his head between his paws and looked up at the boys. Finn had presented his case with such conviction that even Aaron found himself agreeing with some of Finn's more implausible points. He really *would* make a good psychologist. Or maybe a lawyer. Aaron had to fight to keep the sudden grin from pulling at his lips.

"I don't know how I feel about this idea. I can see it being beneficial, but at the same there are liability issues I can't ignore." She glanced at Aaron. "You're not a trained handler, neither of you is, and that's what this dog needs. He needs a stable environment with someone who won't run away from him if he gets a little excited."

"But that's why I said you or Amy would work with us, too," Finn said. "I already thought about that. See? I think of everything."

"Three people at once? That is not only a lot for the dog, but it's a lot of my resources and time for one animal, and we have dozens of others that need work, too."

"I'll work longer shifts once summer starts," Finn argued.

Aaron cleared his throat and stepped forward before Finn dug himself into a hole. "Maria, I know you might not think it's a good idea, but I...I agree with Finn. It makes sense. I think this dog will help me get over my fear. And maybe if he helps me, then I can help him." He hesitated, glancing down at the dog, before looking up at Maria again. "We're both scarred by the past. I'd like to give this a try."

Maria stared at him, then back to the dog. She sighed deeply. "Well, I guess the first thing we need to do is give him a name because I can't stand hearing *the dog, the dog, him, it* over and over. Aaron, will you do the honors?"

❖

"What are you going to name him?" Finn asked as the two of them sat outside in the sun on their short break.

"I don't know yet. What do you think?"

His friend shrugged and sipped his Coke. "It's your decision. I'm not going to give you any ideas because I don't want to influence you. I got to name a kitten my first week here when the litter was born on my shift." He smiled. "I named him Tiger. How original, right? But don't worry about it. If it doesn't come to you today, it'll come to you tonight. You'll be back again tomorrow, and you can name him then."

Aaron nodded and finished his drink. The two went back into the shelter and continued with their work. At eight, Aaron packed his things up and went to Maria's office to say good-bye, but she was already gone for the night and the door was locked. Amy sat at her desk in her small office next door, so he said good-bye to her.

"Have a good night, Aaron. Did you come up with a name yet?"

He shook his head. "No, but I'll think about it tonight."

She nodded. "I'm sure you'll come up with a great name for him."

Aaron shrugged and shouldered his bag. As he turned to leave, the door to the dog kennels caught his eye. It was shut securely, as always, but he wondered how the dog was doing.

Is he scared? Does he feel alone? Do dogs really have emotions like we do? He was sure Midnight had thoughts and feelings, but he'd never really given it much thought. If his cat could talk, what would he say? If this dog could talk, what horrible things would he tell everyone? Or would he only focus on the little kindness that had been in his life?

Shaking the thoughts from his head, he started to head for the exit but stopped once again. The door seemed to call to him, inviting him to step through. He glanced around and, upon seeing the empty halls, turned in the opposite direction and approached. He had never gone through alone, and he knew if he did he would surely be greeted by barking dogs. His palms tingled and his fingers curled into fists at the thought of the ruckus, but he wanted to see if the dog was okay and where they were keeping him.

As carefully as he could, Aaron pushed the door open. A few of the dogs started to bark and sweat began to seep from his pores, but he pushed on. When the door clicked shut behind him, he looked into the many cages. Some held large dogs; others held a few smaller breeds. The doors to the other rooms were shut, and he passed them with his back to the wall so he could keep an eye on the dogs in the same room as him.

Curious eyes followed him as he crept down the corridor. As he neared the end, the volume seemed to decrease as fewer of the dogs reacted to him. In the last kennel, he found the pit bull. He was curled up on the floor in the corner on a plush blanket. A bowl of water and food sat in one corner, untouched.

With his legs shaking, Aaron crouched down and then kneeled in front of the cage just two feet away. The dog raised his head to look at him, his eyes staring into Aaron's. His tail thumped once, twice against the floor before he put his head back down on his paws.

"Poor thing," Aaron whispered. "You've had a hard life, haven't you?" he asked though he knew the dog couldn't respond. "Seems like we're both pretty different from the rest. I know a little about what you've been through. And…I want to help you. Maybe you can help me, too."

Soulful brown eyes stared back at him, and for the first time Aaron noticed more than just the scars on the dog's face and body. His fur was brown with darker brown stripes that made him look almost like a tiger in some ways. The pattern of his fur was interesting and kept Aaron mesmerized. For a moment he even forgot his fear; he had never seen a dog like that, and he wondered how anyone could want to hurt such a beautiful creature.

"You deserve a second chance," he told the dog as he put his bag on the floor and took out a sheet of paper and pen. On it he scribbled *Chance* and stood. A small peg for a clipboard jutted out from the cement block next to the door, and Aaron rammed the paper so the peg stabbed through it. The edges of the paper folded down, but the word stood out in bright blue.

"I hope we become good friends, Chance."

CHAPTER EIGHT

After he woke the next morning and prepared himself for the day at the shelter, Aaron decided not to bother telling his mother about the plans he had, involving Chance. He wanted to see how it worked out before telling her, so he wouldn't feel like a failure if he couldn't handle it. He made sure he kept up the usual chatter at breakfast so as not to pique her suspicions and then took off shortly afterward.

Pulling into what he had designated as his spot, he put the car in park and stared at the building much as he had the first time he visited. This time would be different, though. Nervous energy filled his body and left him tense, but with a sense of anticipation, as well. His palms began to sweat and he wiped them on his jeans before shutting down the engine and climbing out.

Sandra greeted him with a smile as he strode purposefully toward Maria's office. She was looking at paperwork, so he knocked on the frame to get her attention.

"Good morning, Aaron. How are you?"

"I'm good. Ready to get started."

"Great. Chance will be happy to see you, I'm sure. Great name, by the way."

Aaron smiled, relieved. "I'm glad you think so. I visited him before I went home last night and…it came to me. It seemed to fit."

"It does. This is his second chance at life, so let's make it better. But before we start to work with him, he needs to pass the SAFER test. We're going to give him another twenty-four hours to get settled."

She rose and gestured for him to follow. They collected Finn from the cat section on their way and passed through to the dogs. Aaron tensed at the barking but tried to block it out as they passed the cages. They turned a corner to get to the section where Chance was being kept.

"We moved him this morning. It's a little quieter here and it's right by the back door, so we can get him outside without having to pass the other dogs."

"Great name," Finn added, clapping Aaron on the back. "Fits him perfectly."

Aaron nodded and crouched down in front of the cage. "What are we going to do with him?"

"Well, we'll wait another twenty-four hours like I said, and then I'll administer the SAFER test with Amy. The vet came in last night to check him out, though. Overall his health is good although he is underweight, so we'll have to fatten him up."

"I never did ask what the SAFER test is," Aaron said, back pressed flat against the wall as he watched Chance in his kennel.

Finn stepped in. "It's a test given to all dogs when they come into a shelter. It tests them for a few things, like food aggression, sensitivity, eye contact, behavior with toys and other dogs."

"How do you think Chance will do?"

"I think he'll be fine, but we'll see tomorrow."

"Was the bowl empty this morning? He hadn't eaten yet when I left."

Maria nodded. "He didn't immediately go after it, but it was gone this morning. He's a good boy, but he's cautious right now. I think he's probably not too sure what to make of this whole situation, which is why it's best to put off the assessment until Chance is more familiar with his surroundings. Come on. We'll have you and Finn work with the cats today. Lots of work to get done."

Aaron stared through the chain-link gate and watched Chance. He was sitting up today, watching them as they crowded his cage. He didn't approach them, but he didn't seem to be cowering, either. Finn tapped his shoulder.

"Coming?"

"Yeah," Aaron said and, with one last glance at Chance, followed Finn to the cattery.

For the remainder of their shifts, Aaron and Finn cleaned the cats' cages, changed bedding, fed them, and played with them. Finn made notes in the supply room for the items they were almost out of and delivered the list to Maria.

❖

"What are we going to do with him today?" Aaron asked that Sunday morning after he arrived at the shelter. Maria and Amy had already done the SAFER test with him and he had passed nearly all of the areas with flying colors.

"Well, first we need to get him used to human contact. We'll take him for walks, play with him, and make sure he's getting attention. The groomer came in this morning and gave the handsome guy a nice bath, which he seemed to like. After some time we'll introduce him to other dogs and see how he handles it."

"That part of the test he failed," Finn said, frowning.

"Failed? How? Is that bad?"

"No, his reaction wasn't bad, but it's not what we want in a dog. We want dogs to be social, and he pulled away when we brought another dog into the room. Many shelters won't adopt out dogs if they show signs of dog aggression," Maria clarified.

"But if he pulled *away* that shows he won't attack, right? Wouldn't that make him submissive?"

"Right, usually. But if pushed enough—"

"I don't see that happening," Aaron interrupted, surprising himself. *Am I really standing up for a dog?* "Look at him. Look at what he's endured. I think if he was going to attack other dogs he wouldn't look like that."

"You're probably right, but we have protocol to follow, regardless. We can take him outside for a while and bring him into the enclosure to walk him. He does very well with a leash. So far we've seen little resistance, but I have yet to see him walk off leash." Maria pulled a thick red nylon rope off a nearby wall. Chance watched her as she opened the door to his kennel and walked in slowly. She spoke softly to him as she approached and clipped the end of the leash to his heavy collar. "That's a good boy, Chance. Good dog."

"It's important to talk to an animal calmly," Finn explained as she led him to the opening, "because it gets them used to your voice. And by telling him he's good and calling him by his name he'll get to learn what he's called now, and that's something he'll hopefully associate with pleasant things."

"I wonder what he was called before," Aaron murmured, backing up as the large dog came through. His nose sniffed at the air and he looked around at the three people surrounding him, but his eyes seemed to pause on Aaron.

"What he was called before doesn't matter. He's getting a second chance and deserves a new name that will fit him as a good pet. No more bad memories for this boy."

Aaron followed the two of them as they walked out the back door into a large, fenced in area. There were no dogs out at this time of morning, and the ground was clear of debris. Across the large enclosure was another fenced in area covered in concrete. It was much smaller and looked less inviting for dogs to play in, but they couldn't go very far if let loose in there.

"Aaron, why don't you take the leash?" Maria asked, stopping and holding it out to him. Aaron stared at the end of it, waiting for it to come alive and bite him like a snake.

"It's okay," Finn said from his side. "We're here. He won't do anything."

He finally nodded and reached out a trembling hand, firmly grasping the looped end and keeping it from falling to the ground. Chance paid no attention to who was holding on to him as he sniffed at the ground. He started to walk forward, following a scent, and Aaron walked behind him.

When he started to veer off away from the enclosure, Aaron cleared his throat. "Ch-Chance, back this way. Good boy," he added when the dog stopped at the end of the leash and looked toward him. He pulled in that direction again, and Aaron wanted to follow, but Maria stopped him.

"Don't let him take the lead. Gently let him know you're in charge. Just put some gentle pressure on the leash, and let him know he needs to go with you."

"He's strong," Aaron argued as he gently pulled toward him. The dog didn't budge; he spread his stance out and leaned forward, nose to the ground.

"Well, he is a pit bull. They're a strong breed. Tell him to come. Firmly."

"Chance, come," he said as he pulled again. This time the dog looked up at him and took a single step in his direction. Aaron stepped backward and was followed yet again. "Good boy."

"Hey, you'll be a pro at this in no time!" Finn encouraged, giving him a thumbs up. Aaron smiled, pleased with the praise. He lost his focus on the dog for just a moment, and when he regained it that brown face was just inches from his hand, sniffing. His body stiffened in reaction to the attention and proximity.

"Don't back away. Don't show you're afraid," Maria said as she stood her ground right behind him. Aaron nodded slowly, trying to relax, and let the dog sniff his hand. The cold, wet nose touched his skin, and he forced his feet to stay on the ground.

"G-good boy. Good Chance."

Chance looked up at him and sat down, staring into his eyes yet again. There was intelligence in there. He understood. Aaron breathed a sigh of relief. His knees felt like jelly but he was okay. An actual dog—a pit bull, no less—had touched him and sniffed. No teeth were bared and everything was all right.

"Come," he commanded, leading him toward the enclosure again. This time Chance followed him, his tail wagging slowly from side to side as he trotted behind Aaron.

Maria opened the gate for them, and Aaron led Chance in. He brushed his hair from his eyes and stared down. "What do we do now?"

"Get to know him. Let him sniff your hand again and try petting him. He won't bite you, but go easy. Show him you won't hurt him when you touch him and remember to speak gently."

Aaron did everything he was told to do and let Chance sniff his hand more. He murmured what he hoped were soothing words, and when the canine lost interest in smelling him, he raised his hand and put it gently on the dog's head.

The fur was short and smooth, and it felt almost like a baby's skin under his hand. He stroked it gently, thinking about how different it felt compared to Midnight's sleek black fur. When his hand came to one of the scars, he paused and then ran a finger gently over it. Chance didn't flinch as Aaron traced the scar from his eye to the corner of his muzzle. The scar tissue was thick and in places smoother than his fur. In others, where the job fixing him had been inadequate and amateur, the tissue was rough and bumpy. It felt like his, in some ways, and he found yet another similarity between them.

"Poor Chance. Good boy. Who would want to hurt you?" he whispered and let his fingers slide over his broad skull to his neck. The collar was large and looked heavy, but Chance was a strong dog. The smooth fur continued over his back, as did the scars. It felt the same everywhere, but still Chance didn't flinch. After a moment, he sat and wagged his tail while Aaron gained confidence and kept his touch on the dog.

The trust that Chance gave, despite his rough life up until that point, inspired trust in Aaron. If this dog, who'd been so brutally victimized, could let another human touch him, then he could give that same opportunity to a dog. But it wouldn't be any other dog, he decided. Chance was the only one he would work with. He wanted to give this dog another life and make up for the abuses of his previous owners. If he could, he would handpick the family that adopted him and make sure they lavished him with love and affection daily.

"Are you okay, Aaron?" Concern colored Maria's words, but he nodded in response to her question.

"I'm fine." Aaron set the leash on the ground and placed one hand on Chance's side and the other on his back and ran both hands over him simultaneously. As if bored with the whole affair, Chance yawned widely and leaned into Aaron, pressing his warm side into his leg. The dog was heavy, and Aaron shifted his balance to keep from falling over. When he moved his hand back up to Chance's head, the dog pressed into it, using his forehead to nudge into his hand.

"It seems like he likes you," Finn commented, grinning. He sat on the ground and patted it. "Here boy, come, Chance."

The dog didn't budge from his spot. He just pressed harder into Aaron's hand, a low grumbling coming from his throat. Aaron jerked back, but Maria shook her head.

"It's okay. He's not upset. That noise is to tell you he's pleased. Think of cats and the way they purr."

Aaron nodded and returned his hand to Chance's side, stroking one ear gently, then the other. When Finn called to him again, Chance looked in his direction but still refused to move.

"I don't think he understands commands," Aaron stated.

"We'll teach him. By the time he gets adopted, he'll be the most well-behaved dog out there," Finn replied with assurance.

Maria smiled at Aaron. "I'm proud of you, Aaron. I know how difficult this must be for you, but you're doing amazing. Do you think you'd like to work with some of the other dogs as well? Those you could spend some time alone with?"

Aaron shook his head. "No...just Chance."

"But for now, we can't let you spend time alone with him, because of—"

"I know, because of liability. I don't want to work with anyone else right now, though. I feel...I don't know, safe around him. It's strange. I don't understand. I still feel like I'm afraid of dogs, but this one...is different. Finn mentioned how we had some similarities, and I guess we do." He shrugged and patted Chance's head gently.

Maria nodded. "Sometimes people and animals form instant bonds. I just hope you'll be okay when he's ready to go up for adoption."

Aaron smiled faintly. "Finn already warned me about that, and I lost Little Dipper. I think I learned my lesson."

"That quickly?" Finn snorted. "I doubt it."

CHAPTER NINE

"Mom! I'm home," Aaron called as he dashed into the house and threw his bag on the counter. He toed off his shoes and ran into the kitchen in the back, smiling. His mother's iced tea was sitting on the counter, but she wasn't there. The screen door, however, was slightly ajar and Midnight sat by it, the tip of his tail twitching as he watched something outside.

"Oh, no you don't," he said as he picked the cat up and cradled him. "You're not getting outside." He set him down in the other room before heading outside, where he found his mother at the grill.

"Hi, Aaron. I thought I'd fire up the grill for hot dogs. How does that sound for dinner?"

"Fine," he replied. "Sounds good. Guess what happened at the shelter today," he demanded as he sat down in one of the plush chairs. The cushion was faded to a dull brown, but despite its age, or maybe because of it, it had not lost its comfort. He practically bounced in the old seat, eager to share his story.

"I always guess wrong, so why don't you just tell me what happened," she said with a slight smile on her face.

"The other day the shelter took in this pit bull that was used as a bait dog," he started, and then continued with his story. He told her all about how he walked into the room and how he freaked out when he saw him. He brought up Finn and his idea and how he was skeptical at first but ended up naming him Chance. When he told her what happened that day, the look of concern that had been present faded from her face, and her lips twitched up into a smile once again.

"You sound like you did a fantastic job with this dog."

"Oh, the work isn't over."

"I know that. But I meant your attitude. You've changed since you've started volunteering at the shelter. You're more positive about some things. I see more...confidence in you."

Aaron felt himself flush and shrugged. "I don't know if I'd say that. There's still a lot of time left. But after giving him that name I felt a stronger connection to him, aside from the scars. I think he'll be a really good dog for some family to adopt. And maybe he'll teach someone else not to be afraid."

"How do you feel about other dogs, though?"

His stomach knotted at the thought of the other dogs. They were so loud, so energetic. He broke out in an icy sweat as, in the distance, he heard a dog bark. Blood rushing in his ears, he clenched his fist, gripping the cushion he sat on, and pushed away the negative thoughts.

"I just want to focus on him, right now. I can't spend time alone with him, but the other dogs get attention from other volunteers. He needs it the most. He needs *me*."

His mother nodded and faced the grill to turn the hot dogs. "Well, it sounds like amazing things will happen. Why don't you go call Dad and let him know all about your day? I'm sure he'd be happy to hear about it." She gave him a smile. "Dinner will be ready in about five minutes, okay? So don't take too long."

"Sure. Thanks, Mom." Giving her a quick hug, he turned and dashed into the house and took the phone up to his room. When he dialed his father's cell phone it went straight to voice mail, so he left a message for him to call back, saying he had something exciting to tell him. With a few minutes left he picked up the small mess in his room then joined his mother outside for dinner.

"Are you planning on staying at the shelter and volunteering over the summer?" she asked as she set the plate on the table. "You can get a job now that you're sixteen. It might be good to start saving up for college."

"I want to stay at the shelter. Maybe I can pick up a job, too, but I like working there so far."

"Make sure you plan some time for fun, too. You and Finn can hang out and do whatever it is you teenage boys do."

"Finn might be working a lot. He's saving up for school."

"He can't work every day, even if it is summer. You'll find some time. Or you could find a boyfriend."

Aaron nearly choked on his bite of food. "Mom!" He swallowed and sipped his drink. She was right, though. Maybe he could find a boyfriend this summer. The possibility was there—if he could work up the courage to speak to someone.

The two ate their meal in silence, and afterward he offered to clean up so she could relax. She disappeared with another iced tea into the living room and shortly he heard the television tune in to a comedy. He washed the dishes and put them away, then retreated to his room.

His father still had not returned the call, so he powered up his laptop and sat down in front of it. Opening Google, he typed in *pit bulls* to see what information he would find. The first thing he noticed was that the term *American pit bull terrier* kept popping up. When he clicked on it he learned that pit bull is just a blanket term for a few breeds that share similar physical characteristics. Articles on pit bull attacks came up near the top of the list under *news sites*, but he skipped them, looking for other information on the dog. Of the breeds shown to be pit bulls, Chance definitely had to be the American pit bull terrier, and he learned that the strange striped pattern on him was called brindle.

Hours passed, and the sky turned dark outside as he read article after article on proper training, breed characteristics, responsible ownership, and jobs the breed had been used for in the past. He was amazed to see that there had been pit bulls trained and used to rescue people, as well as used for therapy. When he read that, it gave him hope for Chance.

"He would make a perfect therapy dog someday," he said to himself, then took out a notebook and turned to a fresh page. He jotted down some of the most interesting information and set it off to the side to bring with him to the shelter the next time he worked.

According to different articles he read and sites he visited, Chance would need a lot of exercise to keep him fit and out of trouble.

Dog parks seemed to be out of the question, but like Maria had said, socialization was recommended. He tapped the pen anxiously on the notebook as the corner of his lip pulled down in a frown. If the pit bull had been a wildly popular dog at the beginning of the twentieth century, as some of the sites mentioned, why had that changed so much? He couldn't find an answer. He did, however, find an article on a native Connecticut pit bull named Stubby, the most decorated war dog from World War I.

Yawning, Aaron glanced at the clock and was startled to see how late it was. His mother had checked on him at one point, but he'd dismissed her with a wave of his hand. Now it was after midnight and he had school the next morning.

Shutting down his computer, Aaron stored the notebook and climbed into bed. He wouldn't get to see Chance until next Saturday because he had a GSA meeting Friday after school. Until then, there were a lot of things he needed to research.

And his father still hadn't returned his call.

CHAPTER TEN

Two weeks after his argument with Caleb, Aaron started to feel uneasy about his relationship with his two ex-friends. Nothing was overtly amiss, but *something* was wrong, even if he couldn't see it. In between classes, he caught glimpses of Caleb in the hallways. Nothing seemed wrong until the one time he saw Tyler with him. Tyler had glanced over and given a short wave in Aaron's direction. Aaron had raised his hand to return the greeting, but before he could, Caleb had swooped in and whisked Tyler off.

What the hell is his problem?

Thinking back on it, he hadn't seen Tyler since before that Sunday he went over to Caleb's house. Something must have happened, but no one told him.

Friday after school he slipped into the library with his bag and waved at Will and Clarissa before taking his usual seat at the GSA meeting.

"How's work going at the shelter?" Clarissa asked, sliding her chair over to include Aaron in her conversation.

"It's good," he said, glancing up from the notebook he had pulled out with his notes on Chance. "I'm having a lot of fun."

"Meet anyone?" she teased.

Aaron shrugged, trying to look nonchalant. "This kid from Eastern. Name's Finn. You know him?"

Both of them shook their heads.

"Don't know anyone named Finn, but that's a hot name. Is he hot?" Will asked, grinning.

"Yeah, but he's straight."

Clarissa laughed. "Or so he says."

Aaron flipped her off. "He's straight. I checked."

Vicki, Jason, and Miguel entered the library together, laughing about something. They sat down at the head of Aaron's table and nodded to everyone else.

"Angelo can't make it today," Miguel said, pulling out his journal to take the notes of the meeting. "Mom needed him at home."

Vicki nodded and opened the meeting. "Is there anything positive from the last week anyone wants to share with the group?"

Aaron wanted to tell them about his progress with Chance, but he hesitated. He wanted to do more than just pat his head before he announced it. It wasn't like the others would find his experience to be progress.

"I got the job I applied for at Valerie's Salon," Clarissa announced.

Will snorted. "I should hope so. She's your aunt!"

"Hey! It's still a job and it is good news, right?"

Vicki just smiled. "Congratulations. Anyone else? Aaron?"

Put on the spot. Damn. He took a deep breath. "The shelter is going well. I've been working with the cats and…got to hold a puppy." Miguel let out a whoop that earned him a glare from the librarian, even though it was after-hours.

"Dude, that's awesome! Congrats, man."

Everyone else agreed and added their congratulations as they went around the room.

Throughout the meeting, Miguel's hand flew across his page as he took the minutes. Vicki led the group in discussions for end-of-the-year festivities, and Aaron realized they had just a few short weeks left of school. It amazed him how quickly the year had gone by.

And how much had changed.

"These are all great," Vicki said. "I'm glad we've set plans in motion for the rest of the year, and we have some things in the works for next year, too. I spoke with the advisor for our feeder school, and the GSA down there is much larger than usual. We'll get quite a few freshmen next year, even if they don't all join."

"Bigger is better," Jason commented with a snort, which earned him a smack on the arm from Clarissa. "Ow! Hey!"

"Perv."

"I didn't mean it like that."

Vicki ignored them. "Anything else anyone wants to add?"

Will looked nervously around at the group. Aaron watched him assess everyone before he raised his hand just the smallest bit to get their attention. "I had a run-in with some guys in the locker room again."

"What kind of a run-in?" Miguel wanted to know, setting aside his writing.

"The usual. *Stop looking at me, fag. Go change in the girls' locker room.* Other stuff."

"Did you report it?" Clarissa asked.

"What's the use? I've reported it before and Mr. Kingston never did a thing about it."

"Report it again. If he's not going to do anything about it, we'll go straight to the principal. You know he has no tolerance for these things," Vicki said.

Miguel frowned. "Don't know why you wouldn't start with him in the first place."

"It's not too late to report it," Jason added, glaring at Miguel. "I'll go with you tomorrow morning, and you can talk to Mr. Kingston. I've got your back, man."

Will reluctantly agreed, and Aaron glanced around at the rest of the group.

Caleb and Tyler used to have his back. Not anymore, though. Not since he'd come out to them, but this group of friends did. What about Finn? Would he have his back like Jason had Will's?

While he was getting ready for bed later that night, he received a text from Finn. *My car won't start. Is there any way you could pick me up tomorrow?* Aaron replied that he would, and Finn sent his address along with his thanks. He smiled as he climbed into bed. He was curious about Finn's apartment. He wondered if his friend would be waiting outside or if he would get a chance to see where he lived.

Aaron woke up earlier than usual the next morning and found a text from Dad apologizing for not returning his call from the previous weekend. It said to call him when he was on a break from the shelter and left it at that. He hoped everything was okay—it wasn't like Dad to not return calls right away. It was even stranger for him to send a text.

Mom was still sleeping when he poured a bowl of cereal for himself and ate it in front of the television. The news reported the same things as usual. The weather was going to be hotter than yesterday. A murder occurred in the next city, and the suspect was being questioned. He paid little attention to it as he finished the food, turned the television off, and brought his bowl to the kitchen. Just in case his mother woke and wondered where he went, he jotted down a quick note for her explaining Finn's situation and left.

The apartment building Finn lived in on the other side of town wasn't as kept up as it should be, as if the landlord never came around. The sparse grass had grown long and looked unkempt. Bits and pieces of trash littered the spiny bushes that stood sentry over the doors. One of the windows had been broken and was patched up with duct tape. No parking spots were open, so he parked along the curb and waited, hoping Finn would show soon; his desire to see where his friend lived was stamped out.

He didn't have to wait long. Finn burst through the doors, taking the steps two at a time with his bag slung over his shoulder. He practically jumped into the passenger seat and slammed the door shut. "Let's go," he said with no other greeting or smile.

Aaron obeyed and put the car in gear. When they were down the street and on the main road, he finally spoke. "Is everything okay?"

Finn sighed and leaned his head against the window. "I woke up to my parents fighting again. I just couldn't take it. It's not a pleasant way to come out of a dream."

Glancing over at Finn, Aaron noticed the pursed lips and narrowed eyes. He felt hollow inside, like someone had scooped out a large piece of his chest, and he found it hard to breathe. What must that be like, to live in a house like that? Anything he said to Finn would be inadequate. What the hell do you say to a friend who's going through this?

"I'm sorry," he said, though the words felt useless. "Do you have other family around here that you could live with?"

"No. And even if I did, they wouldn't take me in. They'd have to deal with my parents, then. I just can't wait to get to the shelter."

Aaron let the subject drop, wondering if there was a way he could tactfully bring it up later, once he found the right words. After a long, heavy silence, he cleared his throat. "Hey, so I was looking up information on pit bulls this last week."

"Yeah? What did you find?" Finn still seemed distracted from his morning, but at least he was talking.

"Well, I learned that Chance's coloring is called brindle."

"I could have told you that."

"I know, but—"

"Cool, isn't it? It's rare on some breeds but it's awesome."

Aaron rolled his eyes. "I'm sure you already know everything I found, but it was new to me. Chance is going to need a lot of exercise, and the sites said he won't be good in dog parks. There was also a lot of information about his breed in the early part of the twentieth century. I had no idea they were so popular. What happened?"

Finn shrugged. "I don't know. Maybe someone got to using them in fights and it became more popular. A lot of breeds were feared at one point or another. You'll have to look more into it."

"I will. But I was thinking Chance might be a good therapy dog after he's trained. One site said they've been used in a lot of different areas, and that they're good for jobs like that. He might inspire some people because of all he's been through, you know?"

"I agree, and Maria might even agree with you, but he might frighten some people because of his breed and scars."

Aaron let out a huff of air and drummed his fingers on the steering wheel. "Then they don't need Chance to visit them."

Finn laughed and shook his head as they pulled into the shelter parking lot. "You don't control who can and can't see a dog, I think. So good luck with that."

The two climbed out of the car and strode into the shelter. They dropped off their bags in the staff room and made their way to the dogs. When Finn opened the door, the barking grew louder. Aaron still flinched, but he felt more confident as he walked in behind Finn. Keeping his eyes straight ahead and his side pressed to the wall, he was able to walk to the end of the room without his legs shaking, urging him to run out.

Chance greeted them today, his tail wagging happily back and forth. When Aaron crouched down in front of the cage, Chance smiled a doggy smile, his tongue lolling out. "Looks like someone's happy we're here." The two opened the cage door and gave him some food. Leaving it open, Finn moved to start the feeding for the other dogs while Aaron stayed behind.

"I know we're not supposed to leave you alone with him, but I'm here so I don't see anything wrong with it," Finn called from a few cages over. "Besides, what Maria doesn't know won't piss her off." Aaron nodded and sat on the concrete floor. Chance stayed where he was for a few moments before walking to his food dish and eagerly chowing down his food.

When he finished he pawed at his water dish and knocked it over, sending the water spilling across the floor.

"Chance! No! That's not good."

"What happened?"

"He tipped over his water dish," Aaron said as he picked it up. Carrying it out, he shut the latch behind him and went over to the faucet to fill it again. He replaced the dish, then sat back on the ground. This time, Chance ignored the dish and approached him slowly, sniffing the air. When he got close, Aaron forced himself to stay relaxed and held a hand up carefully. Chance smelled it and tentatively ran his tongue over his palm. Aaron let out a breathy laugh as the dog continued to take in the scent covering his jeans. When he got too close, his broad forehead bumped into Aaron's chest, and he put his hand out to stroke the short fur.

As suddenly as he'd begun his snooping, he plopped down and rested his head in Aaron's lap with a sigh. The act was so sweet and trusting Aaron's eyes stung from tears. They hardly knew each other, and yet it seemed Chance was ready to trust him completely. When he rolled onto his back, exposing his belly—which had scars Aaron hadn't seen before—he carefully patted the smooth skin and then scratched at it. Just like the day before, Chance let out a grumble of pleasure while one leg kicked twice at the air.

Several long minutes passed as the two spent time together. The flash of a camera jolted him from his total focus on Chance, and he jerked his head up to see Finn grinning with the camera in hand. "I called your name and you didn't answer. Look how cute you two are."

"Thanks a lot, jerk. I wasn't expecting that."

"I know! That's the perfect picture! Candid photo. We can post this on the site and the board up front. Everyone will love it. Chance looks so relaxed, but you have to get up now. Maria said she's bringing a family in to look at dogs, so we need to pretend we're busy." He set the camera down on the counter behind him and thrust a broom at Aaron. "You can sweep and I'll change the bedding."

Taking the broom from him, Aaron swept the aisle between the cages. Around him dogs barked and whined, and while the noise grated on his nerves at first, it started to fade into the background. By the time the family came in to look at their prospective pets he barely noticed the sounds.

"Some of these dogs aren't yet ready for adoption but will be in a few weeks. Others you can take home as soon as your paperwork is cleared. Was there any particular breed you were looking for?"

The woman shook her head, her hand on the shoulder of the young girl in front of her. "No, nothing in particular, just as long as they're good with kids. We do want a dog that's already been trained a bit because my husband works long hours, and he won't be home as much to help out."

"Understandable," Maria said as she began the tour. "Many of our dogs are already trained. Some of them are at an advanced level, but others still need some work. You'll find the information about each dog listed on the wall outside their kennel. Some are great around other dogs and a few take to cats as well, like Rudy here. His owner moved out of state and left him and his feline companion behind. Sadly, they had to be separated."

"Daddy's allergic to cats," the little girl said as she looked at the dog behind the bars.

Aaron continued to sweep and listened as Maria discussed the temperaments of some of the dogs while Finn chimed in to add his two cents. When they got to the end of the row and approached Chance's cage, Aaron heard the little girl make a noise.

"What happened to that doggy? He looks scary."

"That's not nice, Lilly. He just got hurt a little."

A little is the understatement of the year, Aaron thought.

"Chance is a sweet dog, but he's not up for adoption right now. He still has some training to go through before he can go to a good home, though we would be happy to accept applications and keep them on file until he is ready."

"What happened to him?" the woman asked. "Why does he look like that? Was he in an accident?"

The questions irritated Aaron, but Maria answered calmly. "He was attacked by other dogs. Animal Control found him and brought him in."

"The poor thing. What sort of dog is he? I've never seen an interesting color like that. It reminds me of a tiger."

"American pit bull terrier. The coloring is called brindle and we have a few other—"

"He's a pit bull? Oh, I should've been more specific. That's one breed my husband is against. Boxer, pit bull, Rottweiler, and bulldog are out of the question," the woman stated firmly.

Aaron glanced up and caught the look of disgust on her face. He tried to bite his lip to keep the words from slipping out, but like many other aspects of his life, he seemed unable to control them. "Did you know pit bulls were one of the most popular dog breeds in the beginning of the twentieth century? They were great companions for families. Some wartime posters even portrayed Americans as pit bulls that guarded innocent people."

The woman turned to look at Aaron, as did her daughter. Maria waved her hand behind them, signaling Aaron to drop the subject, but he forged on. "Some people even use them today as rescue or therapy dogs. You shouldn't judge them based on what you hear in the media."

Obviously perplexed, the woman's mouth opened and closed like a fish out of water as she tried to grasp words. Her daughter, however, didn't seem to lack any.

"Mommy! What happened to his face? He looks like the doggy."

Aaron tilted his head down so his bangs brushed forward and covered the worst of the scarring. Mortified by the girl's honesty and angry that her mother said nothing, his hands trembled. Finn stepped up next to him.

"Aaron?" Concern and anger warred in his friend's voice, but he couldn't be bothered with it. He needed to get out.

Now.

Without saying anything, he handed the broom to Finn. As the woman finally tried to quiet her daughter, Aaron rushed through the doors to the reception area, passed Sandra, and disappeared into the staff room.

Chapter Eleven

Aaron took his break and waited for the family to leave. He feared Maria coming in and telling him he was fired, that he had broken the volunteer agreement, but he waited for her decision. When she finally came seeking him out, his head hung low, nearly touching the table, and his grip on his can of soda almost crushed it.

"I can understand if you don't want me to volunteer here anymore," Aaron started before she could tell him the bad news herself.

"Aaron"—she sighed, shaking her head—"I'm not kicking you out. But you need to understand something. Families come here looking to adopt. We depend on them to keep the shelter in operation. We can't treat them poorly or we risk losing their support, and if they spread the news, we could lose a whole lot more."

"I understand…I just…couldn't watch her put Chance down like that."

"I know it's hard, and it's good to educate people. But there is a right way and a wrong way to do it. Attacking their point of view is a bad way. Confronting them in an aggressive manner is also a bad way. The things you said were very true—in fact, I'm impressed by your knowledge. However, you can't tell a person how they should or shouldn't judge someone or something. It's not how we do things around here. We were lucky. The woman did find a dog she and her daughter liked, and they filled out the paperwork. With luck, the dog will be going home with them. Had it been another less understanding person, that may not have been the case. We must never risk losing a potential family."

"Understood," Aaron murmured.

"Good. I'm glad we got that cleared up. Now, why don't we take Chance outside and give him the opportunity to stretch out those legs. Finn is going to take the other dogs for a walk and let them out in the pen to play for a while. Chance can have the smaller area to himself."

Aaron agreed and finished his soda. After recycling the can he followed her back through the shelter. Chance waited for him eagerly, and when he saw him this time, he got up and stood at the ready.

"He's really taken to you. That's a good thing. It shows he has the ability to trust people, and it will be easier to get him adopted. Your progress is fantastic, too."

"I did some studying during the week about pit bulls. There were a lot of things on the Internet about dog fighting and attacks. But I did find good things."

"Of course there are good things. No particular dog breed is inherently bad. It all depends on the person who raises them. Dogs learn from their owners. There are a lot of people who don't understand that and think because of a few incidents an entire breed is dangerous. What they see in the world of dog fighting is nothing compared to how many are kept as friendly family pets. And if they have a dog that shows the slightest bit of aggression, they either have them euthanized or dumped off at a shelter rather than take the time to bring them to obedience classes."

Maria continued her discussion while Aaron hooked Chance up to his leash. The dog tried to pull, but Aaron held on to him and told him to stay. When they walked outside, Finn was already out with another dog, and Aaron kept a tight grip on Chance as he led him to the concrete pad.

He wasn't sure if the grip was for Chance's safety or his own reassurance.

The day was warm, and the sun shone brightly overhead. A few clouds drifted by, occasionally blocking out the sun but doing nothing to ease the heat. Chance was let off his leash in the pen and he wandered to the corner where a tree provided a little shade. He flopped down and looked ready to take a nap.

"You'd think he didn't sleep at all when he was inside."

"Maybe that little bit of walking is tiring for him," Aaron suggested, squatting down in the middle of the concrete floor. Chance watched him for a moment before yawning and putting his head between his paws.

"Let me go back inside and get a few toys for him to play with. He might just need some stimulation."

Aaron stayed with Chance while Maria went to get the toys. He lay quietly in the shade and once rolled onto his back, rubbing against something seen only by him. Aaron laughed at the antics and tried calling him over, but Chance ignored him.

"Here. I got a ball, a rope, and some chew toys. Let's see what he does with the rope first." She laughed softly. "If we give him the ball he might fetch but not bring it back!"

Taking the thick, heavy rope in his hand, Aaron swung it around and whistled. "Come here, Chance! Come see what I got for you!"

The dog perked up and followed the end of the rope with his eyes. His tail started to wag slowly, picking up speed as it thumped into the side of the pen. He got up and stalked closer to Aaron, his head down as he watched the movements. When he was within reach, he pounced forward and grabbed the end of the rope with his paws.

The movement startled Aaron and he almost let go of the rope, but he managed to maintain his grip and tugged. Chance pulled, shifting his weight to his back legs as he jerked it.

"Good, he knows he can play," Maria said, crossing her arms and leaning against the side of the pen. Aaron tugged sharply at the rope, but Chance's grip was firm. He growled playfully, his wagging tail giving away his happy mood. When he tried to walk with the rope, he dragged Aaron forward a few feet.

"He's strong."

"They are known for their strength for a reason. Whoever adopts him is going to need to keep up his work on obedience or be really strong. He'd probably drag you down the street if you don't ground yourself."

Aaron planted his feet firmly against the concrete, spreading his legs and bending his knees a little. He pulled back and Chance growled again, tossing his head back and forth. The rope ripped out of Aaron's hands and Chance fell back with it. When Aaron ran to get the end, the dog danced just out of reach and tossed his head in the air as if teasing Aaron with the end of the rope just as Aaron had teased him moments before.

"Chance! You silly pup," he said as he laughed, chasing him around the pen.

His canine friend pranced around, swinging the rope around and not letting Aaron or Maria get close to him. When they were farther away, he would get down into a play bow with his tail in the air, pretending to rest. But the moment they got closer he would run.

Minutes later, both Maria and Aaron were trying to catch their breath. "I think the ball is pointless. I doubt he's going to bring it back," Aaron wheezed.

"Probably not, but it will be fun to see what he does with it."

Taking the ball in his hand, Aaron whistled for Chance again. He stopped, the rope hanging from his mouth and head cocked to the side. Tossing the ball back and forth between his hands, Aaron called to Chance. The brindle dog dropped the rope and trotted over to him to inspect the new object, tongue lolling out of his mouth.

"Oh, so you do want the ball," he teased, throwing it up into the air and catching it. Chance barked once, dancing back on his feet, ready to run. "Catch!" Aaron said as he let the ball fly. It hit the far side of the pen and bounced back. Chance ran after it, nearly crashing into the fence on his way. The ball bounced for a second time before he caught it.

Rather than returning it, he took the ball to his corner and spread out his body, chewing on the ball and leaving a slobbery mess behind.

Maria said, "I think it's safe to say we're not getting the ball back right now. However, based on his response to the toys, I'd say he was a pet before he was a bait dog—he knows what they're for. But we do need to work on his commands. Like sit, stay, drop it."

Aaron agreed. "If he was a pet before, how old is he?"

"The vet believes he's around two years old."

I hope it wasn't two years of torture. Aaron sighed.

Maria tossed the remaining toys around the pen. "Let's let him hang out here for a while. We can get some other work done. Finn can keep an eye on him while you're inside. The laundry needs to be done for the cats, and I'll help Finn with the other dogs. There's a volunteer you haven't met, working with the cats right now. Her name is Savannah."

"Okay, cool. Will you come and get me when you're ready to bring Chance in?"

Maria agreed and gestured for him to go ahead. Aaron waved to Finn as he passed, pulling back nervously when the two small dogs Finn had on the leash barked and lunged toward him. He slipped back into the building and found Savannah already hard at work with the cats. After their introductions, Aaron got started with another load of laundry. It seemed like there was always laundry to do. It was a good thing the loads were only towels though, which made it easy to fold; he hated doing laundry at home.

"I only work on this side," Savannah explained after a few moments of silence. "I have a mild dog allergy."

"And I'm not allergic, but I don't exactly like dogs."

"What were you doing outside, then?"

"There's one that I'm working with," he explained and asked if she knew about Chance.

"Oh yeah, the pit bull. Amy mentioned him to me. To be honest, I don't really care, since I can't be around them and all. I mean, it's not that I like animals being abused or whatever, but with dogs it's just not a priority for me." She paused and looked at him. "Does that make me sound mean?"

Aaron smiled at her. She was sweet, probably about twenty or twenty-one with long blond hair that she wore pulled back in a half ponytail. Her green eyes squinted whenever she smiled. And like all the other volunteers, she was dressed plainly in dark jeans and a brown T-shirt, which was already decorated with long and short cat fur.

"No, it doesn't make you sound mean. I guess everyone just has their favorite animals. It's not like you just said you wanted all dogs to die."

"Right, I'd never say that. So, how do you like it here so far? I work here about two weekends a month. I did more when I was in high school, but now that I'm in college it's different. There's a lot more work, and I have a part-time job that pays the bills."

"What high school did you go to?"

"Oh, I went to school with Finn at Eastern High. He was a freshman when I was a senior. Not that I knew him then. He's a sweet kid. Wish he was a little older, though," she winked.

"Are you seeing someone?"

"No, why? Are you interested?" She bumped him with her hip as she passed by with a basket of freshly laundered towels.

"Uh, not really…" Aaron started, wondering how he should go about explaining. "I'm more into someone like Finn."

"Oh, cool." Savannah shrugged. "You're even younger than Finn, anyway, so it wouldn't work out regardless, cutie."

She laughed as Aaron felt his face flame. He pulled a blue towel out of the basket and folded it before adding it to the towering pile of towels. Savannah moved through the open door into the cattery, and Aaron watched as she pulled out the old towel and wiped down the inside to clean it. She pulled the litter box out as Aaron joined her to fix the towel and add food and water to the cage. When it was finished, they put everything back and moved on to the next cage, which was currently occupied.

"Snowball is my favorite cat here. If I wasn't staying in a dorm and had a place of my own, I would adopt her. She's such a sweet girl." She pulled the white cat out of the cage and set her on the ground by her side. The cat butted her head against Savannah's arm and rubbed against her side as she and Aaron once again started the process of cleaning the cage. "But she's going to get a good home soon, I know it. Who could resist her?"

Aaron agreed and the two worked to finish the rest of the cages. When it was finished, Savannah glanced at her watch. "It's later than I thought. I need to take my break. What time are you here until?"

"Four. Shorter time today, but I'm going to stay until Finn is done."

"Well, you still have about half an hour left. Why don't you go check on that dog of yours?"

Not having realized how late it was, Aaron nodded. Before leaving the cats, he washed up and then went out the back to see what they were doing. Finn was walking two of the husky puppies from the other day, and Aaron felt comfortable enough to approach them.

"I get off at four, but I'll hang out and wait for you so I can bring you back."

"You won't have to wait," Finn said as he let one of the puppies—the first one Aaron held—run over to Aaron. "I talked to Maria and explained the situation to her, and she's going to let me go an hour early. It's not too busy, she said, so it won't be a problem."

"Are you sure? I know how much you like being here."

Finn smiled, dimple flashing. "It's cool. You're being nice enough to give me a ride. I don't want to make you wait too long for me."

Aaron bit his lip as he ruffled the puppy's fur and let him climb into his arms. "Hey, do you think we can hang out afterward? It's still early and I don't have anything to do at home," he finally said, holding his breath.

His friend looked at him and then at the ground. "Well, my parents aren't supposed to be home, so I guess it would be okay to hang out. The apartment is kind of a mess, if you don't mind that."

Is that why he seemed so uncomfortable at dinner?

"I don't mind."

Finn shook his head. "If you say so. My room is actually the neatest in the place. I don't like a mess," he admitted.

Maria interrupted their conversation when she came out. "Let's get Chance back in and settled so you two can take off." Aaron followed her to the pen and laughed when he saw Chance lying on top of all the toys they had given to him. It seemed that he'd claimed them. "We can put them with him in the kennel. We have enough donated toys to go around for now, so he can keep those if he likes them so much."

"Come on, Chance! Let's go for another walk," Aaron called, leaning over and patting his leg. The dog stood lazily and stretched forward, hunching his shoulders to the concrete, and then dropping his back legs to stretch and drag them against the ground. He groaned as he took a step toward them and then turned back to pick up the rope.

"Good boy for picking up after yourself," Maria said as she gathered the rest and then took the rope from him. Aaron clipped the leash onto his collar, and the two of them led Chance back inside and to his cage. They placed the toys in a corner for him, and as soon as Aaron unclipped the leash, Chance went over, grabbed the rope, and brought it back to his bed.

"He's really attached to that toy," Aaron commented, smiling as he knelt to scratch his ears.

Maria laughed. "Dogs get attached to some weird things. Cats too. I had a cat many years ago that loved socks. She literally would find any sock lying around the house and carry it around in her mouth. Annoying when you start losing socks, but cute at the same time."

Aaron made sure Chance had enough food and water before saying good-bye. He hated to leave him behind like this, but he didn't really have a choice. Chance didn't belong to him, couldn't belong to him, but he would make sure he found a good home as soon as possible.

"We're going to work on his obedience and some other things during the week."

"Can I stop in to visit and see how he's doing?" Aaron asked.

Maria nodded. "Sure. Everyone is always welcome to stop by. There's always work to do, too," she added with a wink.

Aaron laughed and said good-bye to her. He headed out to the lobby and talked to Amy, who was working at the front desk, while he waited for Finn to come out. When he did, they both said good-bye and walked out together.

"You ready?"

"Of course," Finn said with a faint smile.

Aaron remembered his father's text and swore silently. He'd forgotten all about calling him. *Oh well. I can call him after I leave Finn's place. I'm sure whatever it is can wait.*

CHAPTER TWELVE

Finn directed Aaron to an empty parking space in a lot near the building but not directly next to it, explaining that residents got mad whenever someone without a parking permit took one of their spots—it was less of a hassle to walk. Aaron simply nodded as they locked the car and walked into the building.

The outside of the building was worn and looked old, and the inside matched. There was no elevator that he could see, though the building was four stories high. The carpet was a threadbare and dirty faded brown. Steep stairs towered above them to their right and Finn took them. "I'm on the third floor," he explained as Aaron followed.

The stairs creaked ominously beneath their feet and the railing to their left wobbled. Aaron made sure to keep his hand off it—he didn't want it to snap off…or follow it over the edge. By the time they reached the third floor, he was panting. Apparently the stairs were not only steep, but clearly he was desperately out of shape.

"This is it," Finn announced hesitantly as he unlocked the door and pushed it open slowly. "Don't mind the mess. Or any weird smell…"

Aaron made a face at him and followed him into the apartment. He couldn't deny it was a mess; the carpeting on the floor was stained and littered with junk. A worn couch sat in the middle of the living room facing a large television on a cheap table that bowed under its weight. The kitchen was attached to the living room, and a small table scattered with papers, cans, and bottles sat off to the side with two chairs. Unopened mail cluttered the counters while a massive stack of dishes overwhelmed the small sink. From what Aaron could see, at least the trash can didn't bulge with garbage. But then, what was the point of having one if it wasn't going to be used?

"I haven't had time to do dishes yet," Finn said quietly after clearing his throat. He gestured for him to follow and pushed his way through the clothing on the floor in the middle of the room. "My parents' room is through that door, this is the bathroom—which I keep clean—and my bedroom is here." The door he opened was chipped, but the other side of it revealed a room that should have been in another building.

The carpet was worn like the rest of the apartment, but it was free of stains and litter. A twin bed stood in the corner of the room with a small bedside table next to it. On the table sat a lamp and a small pile of books. A door that could only open to reveal a closet was next to the table, and across the room, a single window faced the street. A modern-looking desk was set under the window, with the materials on it neatly organized, almost obsessively so, and arranged by height. A three-tiered bookcase sat next to it, the back against the legs of the desk. It was jammed full with books, but like the desk, organized.

"Nice room," Aaron commented, truly meaning it. He sat on the bed and wondered if he should take his shoes off, but when Finn didn't, he left them on.

"It is what it is. I'm hoping to get enough money saved and get a big enough scholarship to get a dorm room in college. I'd like to get away from here."

"Why not shoot for your own apartment?"

Finn shook his head. "Too much responsibility. I need to focus on school, and while it might be cool to have my own place, I'm not ready for it."

"It might be quieter, though. You might get stuck with a horrible roommate."

"That's a risk I could take. Besides, there are ways around it, and other places I could go. I'll be happy just to get out of this apartment."

Aaron ran his hand over the smooth dark-blue bedding and watched as Finn paced back and forth. "You're acting strange," Aaron observed. "Do you want me to head home? Because if I'm making you uncomfortable—"

"No, it's not you making me uncomfortable. I just don't like being here and I don't like people seeing where I live. It's…embarrassing." Finn sighed and sat down on the bed next to Aaron. "I don't usually tell people what my life is like because I try to present myself in a different way. It's not…hiding who I am, though some might say it is, but it's more like I'm protecting myself, I guess. I don't want people to assume that because my parents are the way they are, I'll end up like them. I want to do my best so I can get out of this situation. I don't want people to judge me because of them."

"I think that's admirable, really. A lot of other people would just accept the situation and perpetuate it. You're trying to break the cycle. That's a hard thing to do, Finn."

Finn looked up at him in surprise. "You think that? Really?"

"Absolutely. And now I know why you looked so uncomfortable at my house. I didn't realize…I'm sorry."

"It's okay," Finn said after a moment. "Sometimes it's tough, I guess, seeing the other side."

The boys sat in silence for a few minutes. It wasn't awkward or uncomfortable because a sort of understanding had passed between them. They each had their own problems, and even though they'd only met recently, they would help each other through them. Aaron was glad he could repay Finn for the kindness he had shown when they'd first started to talk.

A sudden laugh burst from Finn's lips, and he flopped backward on his bed. When Aaron looked at him in confusion, he just laughed harder. "What's so funny?"

"I feel like I'm twelve again. I feel like asking *What do you want to do?* and I know you'll say *I don't know, what do you want to do?* It just struck me as funny."

"Well, what *do* you want to do?" Aaron asked with a laugh, which only set Finn laughing even harder.

As they recovered from their laughter—with Finn wiping his eyes—the front door burst open and angry voices filled the small apartment.

"I told you not to buy more of that shit, Allen!" a woman's voice screeched from outside the bedroom. Finn's face turned white and he got up to quickly shut the door. It did little to block the sounds coming from the other side.

"I didn't realize my parents were coming home so early. I thought we had another hour or so."

"Hey, it's no big deal. Do you want me to head home?"

"No…I'd like to hang out. But we'll see how it goes with my parents."

A crash from the kitchen caught their attention, and they sat in silence. "Allen! I just bought that!"

"Shut up, will you! All you do is harass me. I'm entitled to a drink, especially after listening to your shit all day."

Finn sighed, his shoulders slumping. "Dad is drinking again. Maybe you should go."

"Are you sure? You can come with me and hang out at my house."

"No, I need to stay. It's not good to leave them alone together when they're like this."

Aaron stared at Finn for a moment before his lips turned down in a frown. It was deep and he felt it stretch the scar tissue on his face, but he wanted to get his point across. "You're not the adult here, Finn. It's not your responsibility to take care of your parents. They're the adults."

"You think I don't know that? But you don't understand. I need to be here. Trust me."

"If you say so. But if you change your mind, call me. I'll come get you and we can hang out."

"Thanks…you're a good friend."

Aaron nodded and got up. He followed Finn to the door, which he opened cautiously. The battle raged on in the kitchen, and the sounds were amplified as soon as the door stood open. When Finn appeared, the yelling stopped and their attention shifted to him, but whatever words they were about to say halted when they saw Aaron.

"Mom, Dad, this is my friend, Aaron. He's leaving now."

"Your…friend?" his father asked, eyes narrowing.

"Yes, my friend."

Aaron cleared his throat to regain his voice and gave them his best smile—even if he felt they didn't deserve it. "I work with him at the animal shelter. I gave him a ride this morning. It's nice to meet you." *Kill them with kindness, Aaron*, he told himself. "I'm Aaron Cassidy."

Finn's mother straightened up a bit, her face turning red. "Oh, well...hello. It's nice to meet you as well." *At least his mother has some sort of dignity.*

Finn ushered Aaron to the door, nearly pulling him the rest of the way. "Aaron has to get home now, though. Don't you?"

"Yes, right. Mom called," he lied, waving to them. "It was nice to meet you." Finn gave him a shove out the door and pulled it closed behind him.

"You don't have to be so nice."

"I was raised that way." Aaron shrugged.

"Well, thanks anyway. I'll see you on Friday?"

Aaron nodded and grabbed Finn's arm as he turned to go back inside. "Look. If you need to get away for a few hours, just call me, okay? I had no idea...I mean even if you want to get away for the night, just let me know. You can crash at my house. Anytime."

Their eyes met, and the closed expression on Finn's face softened. "Thanks," he said quietly. "I might take you up on that offer someday..."

Aaron didn't want to leave Finn alone to deal with his parents. He'd seen the look on Finn's face when his parents came home, saw his face grow pale. Giving him a gentle squeeze on his arm, he stepped closer, forgetting personal boundaries. When Finn didn't step back, his heartbeat increased and all he could hear was the rush of blood in his ears.

"Aaron?" Finn asked, tilting his head to the side as Aaron took another step closer.

Aaron put a hand on his shoulder and opened his mouth to speak when the confusion that had been present in Finn's eyes cleared suddenly. He smiled gently and reached up, taking Aaron's hand and carefully plucking it from his shoulder.

"Thank you. For being such a good *friend*," Finn finally said, stressing that last word.

Narrowing his eyes, Aaron wondered what he meant until he realized the position they were in, with one of his hands wrapped around Finn's arm, and his other hand held in Finn's. He'd unwittingly backed him up against the wall.

"I'm…I'm sorry," Aaron said. "I didn't mean—"

"It's okay. Really." Finn smiled and dropped Aaron's hand, and Aaron took a step back. "I'll call you if I need to get away."

"Yeah," Aaron replied, backing away farther. He'd gotten caught up in the moment, allowing himself to see something that wasn't there, and he could have destroyed his fledgling friendship with Finn. *And yet, Finn isn't freaking out.*

They said good-bye and Finn went back into the apartment. Aaron lingered outside the door a moment longer, expecting the shouts to resume, but they didn't. When he felt it was okay to leave, he walked carefully down the stairs and headed to his car.

He drove home with the radio off, but the inside of his head was far from silent. Thoughts ranging from Finn's parents to his moment alone with him outside the apartment raged and fought for dominance, but no single notion seemed to stay in focus long enough for him to grasp it, to understand what he was feeling. When he finally pulled into his driveway, he thought it miraculous that he hadn't crashed.

Aaron said hello to his mother and started up the stairs before she stopped him.

"Your father called about an hour ago. He said to give him a call when you get home. He wants to meet you for dinner."

I guess Dad beat me to it. "Sure, I'll call him upstairs."

In his room, he shut the door behind him and dialed his father's cell phone from his own. It rang twice before his father picked up.

"Aaron! How are you doing?"

"Good, I just got home from Finn's house. I forgot to call on my break. Mom said you called. What's up?"

"I'm sorry I didn't return your call the other day. Things got a little…busy around here. What do you say to going out for dinner tonight? Just the two of us. You can fill me in on what's going on over there, and I can tell you what's up here. How's that sound?"

"Sounds great. Want me to meet you there?"

"No, I'll stop by and pick you up. Maybe say hello to your mother."

Really? Aaron pulled the phone away from his ear and stared at it as if his father's face would be visible. "What's going on, Dad?"

His father chuckled. "Nothing. Why does something have to be going on? I'd just like to say hello to your mother, that's all."

"Okay…"

"I'll pick you up in forty-five minutes. Deal?"

"Sure, that will give me time to shower. I'll see you then."

The call disconnected and Aaron stared at the phone as if it had just sprouted legs and arms and began to dance the hula. Something was going on, but he didn't know what. He would, however, find out.

Stripping down, Aaron grabbed a clean set of clothes and dashed into the bathroom. The shower was hot and soothing on his skin, and he washed off the dirt and smells of the shelter. His life had been thrown for a loop lately, and it was unsettling. First, working at the shelter was a strain, and then the thing with Caleb and Tyler. His friendship with Finn was a plus, even if he'd just made some sort of pass at him, and Savannah seemed to be cool, too. Seeing Finn's house made him…uneasy. To say the least. He wished he could do more. But more what? He didn't have clue number one where to even start, but he didn't like seeing people in harrowing situations like that, and Finn was better than the circumstances he'd been raised in. Finn deserved a peaceful home.

Now his father was acting strange.

Maybe he just got busy and couldn't call back, but that had never happened before. *So much is changing,* he thought as he scrubbed the shampoo from his hair. *I need some sort of normalcy in my life or I'll go insane.*

After his shower, he dried off and dressed in clean clothes. His father hadn't arrived yet, so he spent time with his mother watching the news. She seemed at ease and not uncomfortable with his father coming over, and he wondered if they'd discussed it with each other before mentioning it to him. He didn't ask, though.

The doorbell rang a little later and Aaron got up to get the door. His father was ten minutes late, which, again, was unusual. He had always been punctual to the point of being annoying about it.

"Sorry," his father said as soon as the door opened and he had stepped inside. He gave Aaron a hug. "I hit some traffic on the way."

"Traffic? There's hardly any on the route from your place to here."

"I wasn't at home," his father said with a smile. "Hello, Abigail," his father greeted his mother as she came into the room behind him.

"Richard." She smiled and Aaron narrowed his eyes at the two. "How are you? How is work going?"

"Pretty good. I made a few sales recently, so things are definitely looking up."

"That's great news."

"How's the hospital?"

"Same as always."

Before they could continue the small talk, Aaron interrupted. "I think it's great that you two are getting along so swell," he said with a roll of his eyes, "but I feel like something's going on and I'm being left out. What is it?"

"Aren't you being paranoid," his father teased, ruffling his hair. The strands fell into his eyes and he instantly reached up to push them back. "Come on, let's go to dinner. I made a reservation at the steakhouse and I don't want to be too late."

Another item to check on Aaron's list of suspicious things. The steakhouse was a fantastic place to dine, but well out of their price range. But…if his father had sold a few houses recently, then maybe he could afford to treat.

"See you later, Mom. You'll be okay for dinner?"

"I'll be fine, Aaron. Don't worry about me."

He gave Mom a kiss good-bye on the cheek and then joined Dad in the car. The ride over to Robert's Steakhouse was mostly silent except for the radio playing pop music. His father drummed on the steering wheel to the beat of the music, occasionally mouthing the lyrics. It was one of the normal things about the night, and Aaron settled into the seat.

"We haven't gone to the steakhouse in a long time, have we kiddo? I figured we could celebrate a few things tonight."

"What's that?" Aaron asked as he glanced at his father.

"Well, for one, how many houses I've been able to sell. That's a big deal. And you working at the animal shelter. I don't say it enough, but I'm proud of you, son. This is something to celebrate. I want to hear all about it. You said you had something to tell me, right?"

"Yes."

"Well, let's get the best steaks on the menu and talk!"

Aaron agreed, but part of him couldn't help but wonder if there was something his father was still leaving out. Something he was trying to hide, at least for the time being.

The waitress seated them at a table in the corner and handed them the menus. Both decided on the filet mignon and tore into the bread on the table as they waited for the waitress to return and take their order.

"Tell me about the shelter."

"Well…they brought in this pit bull the other day who had been abused. And I've started working with him. They even let me name him. I decided on Chance."

His father stared at him in shock. "You're working with the dog yourself? Already?"

"Well, not on my own, no. Liability issues, because he's been abused by people and other animals. But yes, I am working with him."

"With a pit bull."

Aaron smiled. "With a pit bull."

"How so?"

"Like, what am I doing?" Dad nodded. "Well, I make sure he has food and water when I go in. And then I play with him a little and take him for a short walk. I clean his kennel. Things like that. Maria helps me. And Finn."

"Have you touched him?"

"Of course. It took some getting used to, especially since he has scars like me and he looks a little frightening at first, but Dad, he's such a sweet dog. You should come over and see him. Do you think you'll have time next week?"

"Sure," he said, taking the last bite of his bread and then sipping on his water. "I'm really impressed with you, Aaron. You've made incredible progress and I can hardly believe it. Tell me more about the dog. How did he get there?"

Aaron launched into the story about the day he showed up and who brought him as they waited. The waitress came and took their order then disappeared. Aaron continued telling him about everything he'd done in the last few days with the dog.

They continued their conversation right until the waitress returned with their food. Once it had arrived, they took a time-out from talking to focus on the steaks in front of them. They were as delicious as they had been in the past, and the meat nearly melted as soon as it hit Aaron's mouth. He savored every bite and took in the rest of the people in the restaurant as he ate.

There were a few families there, but most looked like couples out on dates. Because of the higher prices, delicious food, and great atmosphere, it would be a nice place to take someone someday.

If he ever found a boyfriend.

His father cleared his throat to get his attention so he glanced back at him. "There is something I've wanted to talk to you about for a while now, but your mother thought it best to wait for a bit. See how things played out."

"You've been talking to Mom? About what?"

"I, uh…I've met someone very nice," his father said after clearing his throat.

"That's cool. From work?"

"Not exactly. It's not a working relationship."

"It's not? Then what is—oh. You started dating someone?"

"I'm seeing someone, yes. I wanted to talk to you about it in person. How do you feel about it?"

Aaron shrugged and took a bite of his baked potato before answering, "Dad, you're a grown man. You don't need to ask my permission to date."

His father sighed. "I'm not asking your permission. I just wanted to see how you felt about it. It's important to me because you're my son."

How do I feel about it? Aaron frowned as he thought and took another bite of his food to stall for time. After a few moments he looked up to see his father watching him anxiously. "If she makes you happy, then that's cool. I don't want you or Mom to be lonely."

"I'd like you to meet her someday. Soon, I hope."

"Is this thing serious? Because I don't see why you'd introduce your kid to someone unless it was serious."

"Well, I like her. She's a good woman. Her name is Rebecca."

"How did you meet her? How old is she? Does she have any kids?" Aaron found the questions spilling past his lips before he could stop them. His father just laughed.

"Easy, champ. One at a time!" He sipped his water. "I met her at an open house, actually. She came in looking for something small to buy. I started showing the house and we started talking, and, well, we hit it off I guess you could say."

Aaron frowned. "Are you sure she's not using you because of your job?"

"I'm sure. She's my age, but no, she doesn't have any kids."

"Why not?"

"Aaron, that's her decision and it's a rather personal question."

He looked down at his plate sheepishly. "Sorry. Does she know about me?"

"Yes, she does. I brag about you all the time. The reason I brought her up is because she said she'd like to meet you."

"How long have you been seeing her?"

"A few weeks now…"

"A few weeks! And you're just telling me this now?"

His father set the knife and fork on the plate and folded his hands together. "I didn't want to tell you right away because I wasn't sure if it would go anywhere. Now that we've been on a few dates and spent time together, I thought it would be right to mention it. What if I had mentioned it the first time I met her and things didn't pan out?"

Aaron shrugged, but he felt as if his father had been holding back from him. Sure he was an adult and led his own life, but they'd always told each other everything. Hell, he'd been able to tell his father he was gay, right?

"I don't want this to upset you."

"I'm not upset. I guess I'm just…surprised, is all."

His father nodded thoughtfully. "I guess it would be surprising. I haven't gone on any dates since the divorce…but you're getting older, and I think it's time now. Nothing is going to change, Aaron. I hope you realize that. I'm still going to have you visit and I'm still going to call and annoy you and make sure you're doing your homework."

Aaron rolled his eyes. "Thanks." Though a sense of relief flooded through him that Dad wasn't going to change and it would all be the same as before, he couldn't dismiss the nagging suspicion that lingered.

What if he met Rebecca and she didn't like him? Would his father suddenly disappear from his life?

CHAPTER THIRTEEN

Aaron walked into school on Monday morning with his head spinning. He'd hardly slept the night before, and it showed. Dark circles formed under his eyes, and he yawned every few minutes. His English teacher asked if he was all right, and he responded that he had not gotten enough sleep.

It wasn't completely a lie.

He hadn't been able to sleep because thoughts were busy shifting through his mind, fighting for space. They drifted back and forth between his father, Chance, and Finn. Inundated with these thoughts, he woke with a massive headache around two in the morning. He'd even gotten up to take aspirin for the pain.

First there was his father. Out of the blue, he told Aaron he's dating some woman he met from work. While he was happy for his dad, he felt conflicted, too. How could he not be? What did this mean for his relationship with his father? Sure, Dad had said nothing would change, but things wouldn't be exactly the same—inherently. His father would be spending more time with her. Could that be the reason he hadn't called back on Saturday night? Probably. And what if the woman *didn't* like him? Would Dad distance himself more to appease his girlfriend? Aaron didn't want that to happen. Then there was the issue of him liking her. If he didn't like her, would he have to endure her company? Or would his father end it and move on? Would he *want* his father to do that for him? It hardly seemed fair.

Then there was Chance. The dog was the least of his worries, honestly, but he'd invested his time in Chance and wanted to help him as much as he could. He only wished he had more time to give and planned on it for the summer.

And Finn. He had not expected seeing Finn the way he had on Sunday, with his family. It had thrown him. Finn was such a calm, collected person at the shelter…maybe a bit cocky sometimes, but in a charming rather than annoying way. When they went out for dinner, he had been fun and compassionate. Yet in his own home, where someone should feel the safest, he was trapped. He had to endure his parents fighting and turning on him.

Aaron wanted to help him, too, but didn't know how. What help could he even give? He didn't exactly have the resources to get Finn his own place or fix his car. Would Finn even accept his help if he offered it?

And what the hell had he been doing making a move on him like that? He was lucky Finn didn't punch him in the face for getting so close!

Caleb and Tyler passed by his locker as he switched books and ignored him. He glanced at them, a small pang of longing for lost friendships filling him for a moment, but it passed. He did have a few other people he talked to in school, so it wasn't entirely lonely. Besides, he told himself, the purpose of school was to learn, not to socialize.

However, as the two of them neared the corner, Tyler paused and glanced back at Aaron, throwing him a quick look. Aaron caught it and frowned. He seemed almost remorseful. But as quickly as the look had come, Tyler faded into the crowd and turned the corner with Caleb.

Add another thing to my list of worries. Should I have visited Tyler after I saw Caleb? What if I was wrong about him? Aaron shook his head and pushed that image away. No, the two of them did everything together. If Caleb pushed away from Aaron, so would Tyler.

❖

Vicki had called the GSA together to meet that Monday after school. It wasn't unusual for her to change meeting dates or throw in extra meetings if she felt they needed it. Or if something big had come up for someone. Aaron wondered what it could be as he settled into his chair in the library.

A few students lingered after school, no doubt just messing around on the net. Angelo sat next to him.

"You missed the meeting last Friday. Everything okay at home?" Aaron asked.

Angelo nodded. "Mom had a doctor's appointment and needed one of us to watch Graciela. Miguel and I played for it. But he cheated."

"I did not cheat," Miguel said as he took his seat. "It's not my fault you suck at basketball. Practice, man. Practice."

Angelo snapped at him in Spanish.

Miguel grinned and winked at Aaron, then turned to his brother and fired something back just as rapidly. He turned to Aaron. "He's just a sore loser," he said before shooting back at Angelo, "Stick with soccer."

Angelo looked ready to launch himself over the table as the two continued to hurl insults at each other in Spanish, but Vicki broke it up when she cleared her throat.

"Don't you two fight enough at home? Knock it off. Okay, I suggested we meet today because there's been a bit of a…problem… with some other students. I know it's the end of the year, but I just wanted you guys to know what's going on so if you see anything, you can report it."

"What happened?" Angelo asked, sitting up straighter.

Will looked at the table; the freshman looked miserable. Clarissa slung an arm around his shoulder and squeezed him before he spoke up. "Someone decided my locker needed to be…decorated."

"What did they do?" Miguel asked.

"Etched *faggot* into the paint. The custodian tried to paint over it, but you can still see the writing through the paint."

Murmurs of sympathy went around the group, and Jason shook his head. "I have a feeling I know who did this."

"Did you see something, Jay?"

He shook his head again and glanced up at Vicki. "No, but call it a hunch. Caleb left class early before lunch today and you found it when you were getting your lunch from your locker, right?"

Will nodded.

"But…there could have been more people out of class at that time. It's not fair to just point fingers at Caleb," Aaron argued. *Yeah*

Caleb's been a dick, but would he do that to Will? Does he even know *Will?*

"We're not pointing fingers, Aaron. It's just, with the problems you've been having with Caleb and now this—it just seems oddly coincidental."

Aaron nodded and glanced at everyone else. The end of the school year loomed so close, and they hadn't had a single incident outside of the usual locker-room insults since the start of the year. It came as a disappointment that something would happen now, and to Will of all people.

"You gonna be okay, Will?" Clarissa asked.

He nodded. "Yeah, it's fine. I mean, it's not fine, but you know what I mean."

They all nodded sympathetically.

"We'll keep an eye out for you, man," Angelo said, tipping his head toward his brother. "No one's gonna mess with you or your stuff again."

Miguel agreed. Aaron smiled. The upperclassmen had taken a special interest in Will, as the youngest member of the group, making sure his high school experience went as smoothly as possible. Unlike theirs. Aaron remembered the stories Miguel told the group of when he had come out his sophomore year, and the crap he and his brother had taken.

The meeting broke up, and everyone went their separate ways. Since Will couldn't drive, Aaron offered to bring him home, but Miguel and Angelo had already asked. They all walked out together, though, laughing as they went. Aaron felt relieved Will seemed better. He waved to them as he got in his car.

As he left the school parking lot, he noticed Caleb sitting inside his car, watching.

❖

It was a workday for Finn, so Aaron stopped by the bookstore after dropping off his things at home. He had finished the last book he'd purchased and needed another one. But this time he had something specific in mind as he strode into the store.

The same girl greeted him from the counter, and he smiled at her. The scent of coffee drifted through the air, just like the first time he'd visited, though this time it smelled a bit like vanilla. Finn worked in a section close to the front of the store and spotted Aaron as soon as he came in.

"Hey, you're back. Finish that last book already?"

"Yeah, it was good. I came for something else today. Something specific."

"What can I help you with?"

Aaron grinned. "Do you have any books on dog training or pit bulls?"

Finn laughed and shook his head. "I should have figured. Come with me," he said, leading the way to a side section.

The case that held the books on pets was rather sparse. In fact, of the five shelves in the bookcase, only two of them were on that subject. The other three made up the science section. Finn pulled a few books out, looking at the titles and the covers before pushing them back in. He grunted when he finally found what he was looking for and handed it to Aaron.

"This one is a good book for training dogs and general behavior. It doesn't break it down by breed, though. As for books on pit bulls," he said as he pulled another book out, "this is the only one we have in stock. I'm not sure how good it is, but you're welcome to flip through it before you buy it."

"Thanks," Aaron said, holding on to the books. "I appreciate it." The memory of their awkward moment outside of Finn's apartment flooded back to him and he stared down at his shoes.

"Aaron? Forget it, okay?" When he looked back up, Finn smiled at him. "It's cool."

"But I—"

"I said forget it. Friends, right? Hey, did you ever get in touch with your dad?"

Dropping the other conversation, Aaron nodded and filled him in on the last twenty-four hours. He told him all about the dinner and his dad's new girlfriend, but left out the bit about what had happened to Will's locker. "What do you think?"

"I don't know. It could be a good thing, could be bad. If they get serious, she might be your stepmom. Do you think your dad would want to have kids with her?"

Aaron made a face. "I'm sixteen. I think my dad is done with kids."

"Never know, man. He might decide one more is good. You might be a much older big brother."

"Ah!" Aaron held out his hand. He didn't want to think about it. "Go back to work," he said in a light tone. Finn faked a bow and grinned, then turned back to whatever task he had been at before Aaron interrupted.

Aaron watched him for a moment from behind one of the bookcases. He'd always told himself he'd never try to get involved with his friends. Never flirt with them or anything like that, and yet he felt so comfortable around Finn he'd allowed himself to let his attraction show. And yet...Finn did nothing to distance himself. He showed none of the signs Caleb and Tyler had when he'd come out to them.

He smiled and took a step back, away from where Finn was working. He might want a boyfriend, but Finn was definitely not going to fill that role. And that was okay with Aaron.

Before looking at the books, he bought an iced coffee and sat down in one of the plush chairs. The table opposite him was clean, so he put the drink and one book down. He looked first at the dog training book and decided it would be a good purchase. He set it on the table and picked up the book on pit bulls.

A lot of the information was about breed standards, temperament, and training. There was information on the history of the dog, good and bad, and very little else. Aaron read what was interesting to him and made note of it, but overall the book didn't have what he needed. Not wanting to leave a mess for Finn or any of the other workers, Aaron returned the unwanted book to the shelf. He headed up front and had the girl ring him out.

"Did you get a new puppy?" she asked as he handed her the cash.

"What?"

"Your book. Did you get a puppy?"

"Oh, no. I'm just looking into uh, doing some dog training. Research, I guess you could call it." She shrugged and handed him his purchase. Thanking her, he took it over to the other side of the shop to find Finn.

"Thanks for your help. The dog training book is good, but I put the other back."

Finn glanced over his shoulder and nodded. "Anytime, man. Good luck with it. Let me know if you learn anything," he said with a grin.

Though his visit was short, Aaron had found what he came for and walked back out to his car. As he got in and set the bags down, he caught sight of two people approaching the car from the sidewalk. On closer inspection he saw it was Caleb and Tyler.

Had Caleb followed him?

Steeling himself for a conflict, he put his iced coffee in the cup holder and stood, leaning against the open car door and using it as a shield for his body—though he doubted they would do anything, it never hurt to be prepared. Plus, leaning on it casually masked the tension he felt.

"Hey, what's up, guys?"

The two looked at each other, then back to Aaron. Tyler spoke first, pushing his long brown hair from his eyes.

"We heard a rumor at school and came down to check it out."

"What rumor is that?"

"That you're dating a kid from Eastern."

Aaron snorted and rolled his eyes. "I don't even know anyone who would make that up. I work at the shelter with a student from Eastern, but that's it. We're friends."

"That's not what people say."

"Yeah? What people? And why the hell would you even care? It's not like we're friends anymore, is it? Besides, I've hung out with him twice."

Caleb looked like he was about to say something, but Tyler cut him off with a sigh.

"Okay, if you want to know the truth, it was really just an excuse for us to check up on you. Caleb ran his mouth the other week, and I'm sorry about that."

"Hey! Speak for yourself," Caleb argued, glaring at Tyler.

Aaron's mouth dropped open as he stared at them in astonishment. "You…what?"

Tyler sighed again and looked tired. "These whole last few weeks have been a huge misunderstanding. Actually, a lot of the last year has been. And I'm sorry for that. But these last two weeks or so have definitely been Caleb. I don't know why I believe him anymore, honestly."

"Hello, right here, asshole!" Caleb looked at the ground then crossed his arms. "It's not my fault if people talk."

"Again, what people?" Aaron asked. The only people who knew about Finn were the other GSA members.

"Susan saw you at the diner with him. She thought it was a date."

"Well, it wasn't. We were hanging out, just like the three of us used to."

Caleb sneered and spat on the ground. "Yeah, like I believe that. Just hanging out. Is that what fags call it?"

Tyler took a step away from Caleb and gaped at him. "What the hell?"

"So is that what I am now? Let me guess, you *were* the asshole that played Etch A Sketch on Will's locker."

Caleb shrugged. "So? The little punk looked at me in the showers after gym. He got what was coming to him."

"You said you didn't do that!" Tyler said, pointing at him. "Why—"

Aaron cut Tyler off, shaking his head. He felt like an idiot for defending Caleb to the guys at school. "Will wouldn't give you a second glance, man. He has better taste than that."

"You're sick," Caleb sputtered, stepping back. "Tyler, let's get out of here."

"Just go," Tyler said, leaning against the hood of Aaron's car. "I'll catch up with you later."

Caleb stared at them a moment before flipping them off and stalking down the road. He disappeared around the corner and Aaron glanced at Tyler, who stared sheepishly at the ground.

"You know, you've been an ass the last few weeks, too."

"I know, I know. I'm sorry, okay? I've been a total dick about everything."

"You can't just blame Caleb."

Tyler closed his eyes and nodded. "I know. It made me uncomfortable at first, you being gay. But…that's stupid, right? It's not like you'd do anything." He didn't sound so sure of himself, and Aaron felt a stab of betrayal.

"It hurts that you would even think that, Ty. Of course I'd never do anything. That's just…" he trailed off. His thoughts ran to what he'd wanted with Finn and how he'd gotten close to him, hoping that maybe they could have something more.

"I'm sorry. I miss hanging out with you. With just Caleb around, it gets kind of boring."

"All he does is play video games."

"Or talk about Brianna Westley."

"Still?"

Tyler nodded and grinned, and the two of them broke out laughing.

The tension started to fade and Aaron realized he'd misjudged Tyler. "I should apologize, too. I thought you would be the same as Caleb, so when I went to see him the other week…I didn't bother stopping by your house."

"It's cool—I guess the way we've been, it's understandable. I've been a dick. You opened up to us and we shut you out."

"I trusted you guys."

Tyler made a face and shoved his hands in his pockets. "I know. We didn't get it."

"There's nothing to get. I'm still me."

"I know that now. Don't hold your breath for Caleb, though."

The three of them had been friends with each other for so long, then seemed to drift apart. And yet, here he was with Tyler. Did Ty really not hate him? Was it really happening? Or did Tyler and Caleb both have some other motive?

He must have been lost in thought for a moment, because he heard his name and blinked. Tyler watched him intently and had his hand held out. "Truce?" he asked. "Do you forgive me?"

Hesitating only a moment he took Tyler's hand and shook it. "Friends don't need a truce. Just…if you have questions about something, ask me. Okay? It's going to save a lot of grief in the end."

"Deal," Tyler said.

"How did you guys know to come down here?"

"We heard the guy that volunteered at the shelter worked in a shop down here, so Caleb wanted to come investigate. I guess it was just luck we ran into you. We didn't know he was here, actually. Is he?"

"You mean Caleb didn't just grab you after finding out I came here?"

"What?"

"I saw him waiting in his car after school." Tyler digested the information silently, before Aaron answered his question. "Yeah, and his name is Finn. He's cool. He volunteers at the shelter because he wants to be a vet."

"Not my thing, but I guess that's good."

Aaron came around the door and shut it. He propped his body against the car, leaned back, and crossed his arms in front of him.

"How are you managing to volunteer at a shelter if you're afraid of dogs?" Tyler asked. "Caleb told me you just work with cats or something, but that can't be right. Can it?"

"Mostly I work with cats," Aaron admitted. "But there is one dog I've been working with."

"How?"

"Finn had me work with a puppy first. It was hard, yeah, but it was cute, too." He told Tyler what he had been telling everyone else about Chance, and he listened with interest. Aaron kept going and updated him on everything that had been going on with his father, too, and ended with him buying the book to help train Chance.

"Man, you've been busy without us...me. I'm kind of jealous," Tyler said. "I've done nothing but schoolwork. Well, when I get around to it."

Eventually they split ways because they had other plans, but they agreed to meet for lunch the next day at school like they used to— except without Caleb. Part of Aaron wanted to go back in the store and tell Finn what had happened, but he didn't want to bother him again while he was working. As he climbed into his car he sent him a quick text. *Call me when you get off work.*

If things continued in the direction they seemed to be going, Aaron was going to have one hell of a summer.

CHAPTER FOURTEEN

In the five weeks Chance had lived at the shelter, he showed remarkable progress. Almost as much as Aaron. When he couldn't work with Chance for whatever reason, Aaron gradually opened up and started working with more of the puppies, and then the smaller dogs. With Finn by his side, his tremors eased and became smaller shakes that gradually faded until he actually felt able to start working with the larger dogs.

At first, he wouldn't enter the kennel, and then with Finn riding shotgun, he found he could. At first, he would only touch the dogs if they were on a leash that someone else held on to. Finally, he began to take the leash from the others, and then he took the more obedient dogs for walks—with Finn, once again, at his side. Sometimes a second dog would join the trio for a walk as well.

Despite all the extra work, Chance still consumed most of his time. Maria worked hard at socializing him with other dogs while the boys were at school, and so far she had found a small bit of success. With smaller dogs he became friendly, but the larger breeds still made him cower in the corner, tail tucked between his legs.

On the Sunday after Aaron's fifth week there, Maria called him into her office to talk. "Have a seat," she said with a smile on her face. Aaron took the seat directly across from her. "You're not in trouble, so if you're worried, forget about it. I just wanted to see how you're doing and get your perspective on everything that has been happening around here."

"Well, I think I've made a lot of progress with dogs. I'm much more comfortable around them now. I'm proud of how far I've come, and I'm really proud of Chance, too. He's gone through so much, and he's changed just as much as I have."

Maria nodded thoughtfully. "Yes, that's true. Both of you are remarkable. I wanted to let you know how pleased I am with your progress." Her lips quirked up in a faint smile and she rested her chin on a hand as she gazed at Aaron intently. "To be honest, the first day you walked in here, I wasn't sure how it would work out. I thought you'd still be working solely with the cats right now, but you've exceeded my expectations. You proved me wrong. And that's a good thing, because sometimes life needs pleasant surprises like that. As for Chance, he is one incredible, resilient dog."

Aaron beamed with pride. "Yes, ma'am." He laughed a little and added, "Too bad I can't give him a home."

Maria smiled. "It's been over a month since he's been here, and with his progress and yours, I don't see why you can't work with him alone for the rest of his time here. Obviously others will help when you aren't available, but when you are working, his care will be your responsibility. Can you handle it?"

Aaron could hardly fight the grin that fought to split his face. "Absolutely. I won't let you or Chance down."

"Good. I also wanted to let you know first—since you're so close—that next week Chance will officially be going up for adoption."

Aaron's eyes widened in surprise and he broke into a smile. A quick pang in his chest reminded him what Chance being adopted would mean for their friendship, but he tried to push it aside.

"He's a healthy, energetic boy up to his full weight. The vet has given him clearance in terms of any wounds that still needed healing, and he carries no disease. He also continues to show no human aggression and he's comfortable with the smaller dogs. And he's been affectionate with a cat or two," she added with a chuckle. "I think we'll find a fantastic home for him."

Though it hurt to think of Chance leaving, Aaron was glad to know he had improved so much. "He's great. Anyone will see that. I bet he goes home the first week he's put up!"

"Maybe not the first week, but we can hope. Anyway, since you've worked so much with him, I'd like to ask you for a favor."

"Anything," Aaron said eagerly.

Maria laughed again and shook her head. "Always ask before you agree. I would like you to write up Chance's story for the website. I'd like to make him a featured-pet listing and highlight him on our Facebook page. There are some examples up there now for inspiration, but tell potential families the story of how he came to be here and how he's worked hard to be the dog he is today."

Aaron's eyes widened in disbelief. "Are you sure?"

"Yes. I'll check it before I put it on the site. We'll post it with a few pictures of him playing to spice it up a bit. Make him even more appealing."

"That sounds great. I'll get to work on it tonight."

"Thank you, Aaron."

He left her office and found Finn working with a rather large pug, trying to get her to walk before she ate. "Man, this dog is so huge. Her owners definitely cared for her before she ended up here," he said, gently leading the dog. "But then again, maybe not. Obviously they didn't watch this girl's diet."

The pug followed after him, snorting a little as she waddled on her short, stubby legs. Aaron watched in amusement as the pair paced up and down the corridor with other dogs barking around them, begging for attention, before he put the dog back in her kennel and gave her a special diet blend. "What did Maria have to say?" he finally asked once the chain-link gate was locked behind him.

"She wants me to do a write-up on Chance for the website. He's going up for adoption next week."

Finn jerked his head up, grinning. "That's awesome! For both of you! Congrats, man. Do you know what you're going to say?"

"I've got an idea," he said. "I want to make the story personal and make him as appealing as possible. But I want people to know about what he went through."

"Yeah, add something that will tug on the heartstrings. People eat that stuff up like candy."

Aaron went home that night and sat down in front of his computer, logged on, and looked at all the website listings. He also checked out other adoption agencies to see what they had written about their dogs. Some had them listed from the dogs' perspective, others from the trainers' or foster families'. He decided he would just write it from his viewpoint. If he told people how afraid of dogs he had been until Chance, it would make him seem even more appealing. He hoped.

After drafting a listing, deleting it, and starting over, he finally had something he was pleased with, without adding himself to the story.

> Chance is a three-year-old brown brindle American pit bull terrier. He was brought to Happy Endings Animal Foundation one day after animal control found him while investigating an abandoned lot. He was badly injured, scarred, and scared, but they knew this dog was special. He was brought in with no name, but he found a home with the volunteers and staff at the shelter. Though shy at first, he warmed up to those who worked with him, and he is slowly starting to enjoy the company of small dogs.
>
> Though he might look strange, with scars marring his beautiful brindle coat, he is a sweet, affectionate dog who loves to play. He will lick your face at every opportunity and thinks he's as much a lapdog as the Chihuahuas are. He has undergone training and can follow basic commands on and off leash. Because he is a high-energy dog, he needs a family who will take him for lots of walks, let him play in the yard, interact with him, and give him many toys to chew on.

Aaron stared at the final draft and smiled before sending it to print. Maria would be pleased with it. He was happy with the wording and thought for sure it would bring a smile to many faces. This dog had survived, and someone would understand how special that made him.

Chapter Fifteen

Maria couldn't have been happier with the bio/blurb and posted it on the website the next week. She included pictures of Chance sleeping, playing alone outside with his toys, playing and training with volunteers, and even one with him and a kitten. How she got that picture, Aaron didn't know.

After two days of the picture being up and increased interest on the website, Aaron asked if anyone had called. Chance had officially gone up for adoption and he wanted to see him in a loving home.

"Give it some time, Aaron. Fully grown dogs aren't like kittens or puppies. They take some time to find the right home. He'll have his happy ending," she said with a smile.

"I'm just really eager to see him placed."

"I know you are."

"Well…sort of. I mean, I'll really miss him."

Maria smiled with empathy. "While we all will be sad to see him go, he deserves a forever family. A second chance for Chance."

Aaron left Maria's office feeling a little deflated, but his spirits lifted when he saw Chance eagerly waiting for him in his kennel. The dog barked happily and jumped up on the chain-link gate, his tail wagging furiously.

"Hey, buddy, glad to see me?" He reached through and scratched his head before shooing him down. Chance backed up and sat, waiting for the leash with his tongue lolling out of his mouth.

Once Aaron clipped on the leash, Chance tugged once until Aaron gave him the command to heel, and he stopped, obedient.

Aaron felt a surge of exhilaration as he strode out the back door with Chance at his side.

Finn was playing with some dogs in the back, letting them socialize. Aaron kept Chance on his leash and let him sniff around the other dogs. He didn't show any aggression toward them, and while he did seem to want to play, he only showed interest in the smaller dogs.

Allowing him to play while still holding the leash proved to be difficult, but he managed. A young golden retriever approached him, sniffed, and barked at him, eager to play. Chance dropped onto the ground, barking back with his tail wagging in the air. Finn threw them a toy, and the two of them tugged on it. The retriever dropped it and let Chance have the toy after catching a scent and going to investigate.

"How long do you think it will be before someone puts in for him?" Aaron asked Finn as he sat against the building in the small amount of shade, with Chance at his feet.

Finn shrugged and threw a ball, laughing as the retriever, a husky, and a small terrier all chased after it. "Could be days, could be weeks. And I know Maria's already told you that. Don't get your hopes up, but don't give up, either. It will all work out in the end. And stop asking so many damn questions! Just enjoy your work."

"Yes, sir!" Aaron laughed.

The day was cool for early June and cumulus clouds floated across the sky. Some were darker, ominous, and threatened rain where they rose from a larger mass in the distance. As the dogs played or lazed about, the boys talked about the upcoming summer. Aaron was just a sophomore and had plenty of time to think about college, but Finn was a junior. College waited just around the corner for him.

"I think this will be my last really free summer."

"You have the summer after your senior year," Aaron said, scratching a spot behind Chance's ears that caused him to groan in appreciation and roll onto his back.

"I was thinking of getting a jump start on college. It will be cheaper if I take the basic courses at a community college and transfer those courses to wherever I go. But I might be able to get a really good scholarship, and then I'd want to start as soon as possible."

Aaron couldn't blame him for wanting to get out of his apartment, and even though it was still more than a year away, the unavoidable loss of his friend bothered him.

"Have you started applying to schools yet, or is it still early?"

Finn shook his head. "A little too early. I can start in the fall, though. I've been looking at schools. There are quite a few that have excellent veterinarian programs."

"Are you staying in Connecticut by any chance?"

"I doubt it, at least, not if I can help it," Finn said but nudged Aaron gently. "But hey, that doesn't mean you can't drive and visit me. Hang with the cool college kids."

"Do you really think you'll want some high school kid visiting, while you're trying to impress older college women?"

Finn turned and rolled his eyes, then seemed to think twice. "Yeah, okay, the college women will be a plus, I won't deny it, but the program I'll be going into probably isn't very conducive to a long-term relationship. Maybe a few dates…We'll see how that goes when I get there. But I'll still have you visit. I promise. Wouldn't want a girl who judged my friends, anyway."

That comment touched Aaron, but he held on to his skepticism and stood with Chance. "I'm going to take him back inside, do some work in there," he announced.

Finn nodded and threw the ball again as Aaron led the pit bull back inside. His kennel had been cleaned and food and water waited in his bowl, so Aaron unclipped the leash and let him in. He instantly went to his bowl and started to eat. It had taken some time, but Chance had finally bulked up to his full weight and looked much healthier than when he'd arrived. No longer could they see his ribs and hips jutting out.

Aaron worked with the smaller dogs and brought them outside for individual walks while Amy washed down the kennels and gave the dogs fresh food and water. After walking his third dog, Aaron gathered the dirty towels and blankets and started a fresh load of laundry. One had just been taken out of the dryer, and he folded it and put the towels away in the storage unit. He continued working with the dogs, letting some off their leashes to play with whatever dogs Finn had with him.

Although he could work with the dogs now, he made sure not to overwhelm himself and take more than one at a time. He didn't think he'd ever be able to, unless they were puppies, but that was okay with him. A large portion of his fear had dissipated. Enough to allow him to think about other things while he worked, rather than focus solely on the dogs.

Like how Tyler wanted to meet for dinner—a nice gesture.

And how Caleb wanted to tag along—not feeling as great about this.

What the hell did Caleb want? He'd just be a pain in the ass and cause trouble, which made Aaron want to skip the dinner altogether. Friendship triangles could be tricky. Throw in the fact that one triangle point was *queer*, and they ratcheted up to flat-out treacherous. Was it even worth it? He needed an ally—a true-blue, got-your-back wingman.

"Hey, after work is done here today, Tyler is meeting me at the diner for dinner. Do you want to come with us?" Aaron asked when he next saw Finn.

He paused a moment and Aaron knew he had to be mentally calculating how much money he could afford to spend. "Yeah, I guess that would be cool."

"Great!" Since Tyler had apologized to him, Aaron had wanted the two of them to meet. Tyler seemed to have completely changed since the time he'd been avoiding Aaron, and it pleased him. Even with Caleb still distant, Tyler at least backed him up at school whenever he had a problem, and he dropped by nearly daily. His mother seemed skeptical about the renewed friendship at first, and she had cornered Tyler one day and given him some sort of talk. Tyler had walked away chagrined, but to this day Aaron had no idea what she had said to him. Tyler wouldn't let Aaron coax it out of him.

Later that evening, Aaron and Finn met at the diner. Tyler glanced at him sheepishly and then flicked his eyes over to Caleb, who leaned against his car.

"Shit," Aaron swore, shaking his head.

"What?"

"Caleb tagged along. I told Tyler no, but he's a stubborn ass, anyway."

"Oh," Finn said, eyeing the one he assumed, correctly, to be Caleb. "And he's the one giving you trouble?"

"More or less. He's backed off a bit since Tyler came around and stuck up for me. But I still don't know what to do about him defacing Will's locker," Aaron said under his breath as they approached. "Hey, Ty. Caleb, didn't expect to see you here."

"Yeah, well when Tyler decided to cut out early I decided to tag along."

Tyler shrugged. "We were at his place playing video games," he said as if that was a good enough excuse. "You must be Finn." He nodded. "Thanks for helping our friend here get over his fear of dogs."

It was Finn's turn to shrug and he shoved his hands in his pocket. "Didn't do much, really. Aaron did all the work."

"Come on, let's get seats before it gets busy," Aaron said, anxious to get inside. They followed him in, with Caleb bringing up the rear.

Once they were seated and had placed their orders, Tyler started the conversation, trying to include Finn. "So tell us what goes on at the shelter, Finn. Aaron said you've been there longer. Do you have different things you're in charge of or something?"

Finn shook his head and sipped his Coke after it arrived. "I'm considered a senior volunteer, but that's about it. Since I don't have any real expertise I'm not allowed to handle paperwork or things like that. The director, Maria, and full-time staff like Amy handle that area."

"Can anyone volunteer?" Caleb asked, surprising at least Aaron.

"Sure. The shelter is selective, and once you're in the process, you have to undergo a period of observation and then there's an application you fill out, just like at a real job. They have to make sure you're there for the right reasons, and not because you want to do harm to the animals. That might seem strange, but it has happened before. Not at Happy Endings, of course, but elsewhere in the country."

"That's awful," Tyler said, shaking his head. "I have a dog, and my mom and sister both have a cat each, so our house is like a zoo some days. I can't imagine anyone wanting to hurt an animal."

"It happens all the time. Every day thousands of animals are abused. It doesn't make sense to me, either."

Their food arrived and the boys' hunger took over. Aaron bit into his cheeseburger and nearly choked when the grease dripped down his chin. His friends laughed, Tyler and Finn more than Caleb, and Finn tossed him a napkin, which he used to wipe the mess off. The diner began to fill up, and more kids from school filed in. Caleb and Tyler waved to a few, and Finn waved to another, but Aaron kept to himself. Some local families joined in as well, out for a quick meal after a movie or a long day of shopping. Soon the place was noisy and packed.

"I was thinking about getting a job at the mall this summer," Tyler announced loudly to be heard as they moved on to their fries. "Make some cash. I've got a car I can't afford to drive yet," he said in frustration. "No money for gas means no dates with Stephanie."

"So now it's Stephanie you've got your eyes on?" Caleb teased, jabbing his friend with his elbow.

"I thought you liked Michaela." Aaron frowned. "Am I that far out of the loop?"

"It's been a while. Michaela is dating Craig. I've got no chance there now."

Aaron turned to Finn. "Michaela's a hot honors student. Craig is the student council president."

"Yeah, they're like a power couple." Tyler sighed. "Should have seen it coming."

"So what about you? You got a girlfriend?" Caleb asked, addressing Finn. A note of hostility colored his voice, and he raised an eyebrow as he ate a fry.

"No time right now," Finn admitted, either not noticing or not caring about Caleb's sudden attitude. Aaron cared, though. "I work Monday through Wednesday, and Friday through Sunday I'm at the shelter. I had a girlfriend but she was pissed that I spent so much time working."

"You still have Thursday," Tyler pointed out.

"What Finn neglects to mention is his 4.0 GPA."

Caleb and Tyler stared at Aaron and then looked at Finn, eyes wide with shock.

"Holy shit, man. You're like...some supermachine!" Caleb announced, and the tension drained from Aaron.

"How do you manage it?" Tyler asked.

Finn shrugged, glancing sheepishly at his plate. "I know what I want and I push myself to get it. It's not that big a deal, really."

"And he's modest, too," Aaron teased.

"We're lucky you don't go to our school. The girls would be all over you," Tyler said, frowning.

"You'd be surprised," Finn replied.

The conversation turned lighter as Finn told them about the classes he had at his school, and they commiserated about tough teachers while they finished their meal. Though they were stuffed, when the waitress asked if they wanted dessert, all four ordered sundaes to stay longer.

"We get out of school in less than two weeks," Caleb announced suddenly as he scraped the bottom of his sundae dish. "Anyone else excited?"

The three of them agreed.

"My family is going up to Maine again. Three weeks this year, in August. I want to go, but if I have a job I don't think I'll be able to," Tyler said.

"Can you go for a week and just drive back yourself?"

"I don't think my parents will want me doing that. I've only had my license a little longer than you," he pointed out, "and that drive is over three hundred miles, I think. I haven't driven longer than half an hour."

"The sacrifices we make as we get older," Caleb said as he clapped his friend on the back.

The waitress delivered their check, and the boys pulled out various amounts of cash for the tip and bill. Tyler went up to pay and left the extra on the table as they all filed out of the booth and headed out to their cars.

"See you tomorrow in school," Tyler said as Caleb got in his car. Finn and Aaron lingered a little longer.

"What did you think?" Aaron asked when they were out of hearing range. Finn glanced in their direction and shrugged noncommittally.

"They were all right. I still don't like that they ditched you before, but if Tyler's moved past that, then I guess it's cool. Caleb's an ass, though."

"Yeah, well, I'm not exactly thrilled with Caleb, either. I don't know why he tagged along but at least he behaved himself. Mostly. I'm going to talk to Tyler about it, though."

"Why?"

"Because he's still hanging out with him. After the crap he pulled and the shit he said? If Tyler wants to be my friend again, wouldn't it make sense to ditch him?"

Finn shook his head. "Yeah, it's not right, but if they're still friends…as long as he doesn't let Caleb get away with saying shit, then you kinda have to let it go."

Aaron frowned and rubbed at the scars on his face. *How can I let it go? It hurts.* "Anyway, I'm glad you got along with them, or at least Tyler. It would be awkward to hang out if you didn't."

Finn grinned. "I get along with pretty much anyone, Aaron. As long as they're good people and aren't being total jerks, it's cool."

Aaron breathed a sigh of relief as they parted, though he couldn't help but think matters with Caleb weren't settled.

CHAPTER SIXTEEN

The final two weeks of school passed in a blur for Aaron. Exams came and went. Teachers handed out summer assignments. The seniors got ready for graduation, but he knew no one who he wanted to keep in touch with once they left. Tyler was heading out for a weekend at the beach and invited Aaron along with Finn and, unfortunately, Caleb, but Aaron had work to do at the shelter and declined.

Finn kept busy, too. Maria had planned for a fundraiser and adoption event the week after school let out. He had been placed in charge of getting photos of all the animals and creating an inviting display. He and Savannah also typed up reports on each of the animals under Amy's supervision. Aaron didn't know what went on during this sort of event, but Maria filled him in.

"We're a nonprofit organization and we rely largely on donors to keep in operation. This fundraiser we do twice a year—once in the summer and another around Christmas. We invite anyone from the community but especially those who have been instrumental with helping in the past. It's also a great opportunity to show off the animals we have and get them adopted."

"How does that work?" Aaron asked, curious.

"It draws attention to the shelter, so people who may not be completely convinced they want to adopt stop in, just to look around. Last year was a huge success, and during that event alone we placed nearly two dozen cats and kittens, and about ten dogs."

"In one day? That's amazing!"

Maria nodded agreement with Aaron's enthusiasm. "We also raised enough money to keep in operation for a couple of months without having to worry about the budget. It might not seem like a lot, but it gave us plenty of room to work with for leaner times. We also usually get a lot of donations in food, toys, and supplies."

"Wow! That's awesome," Aaron commented, amazed.

"Right. And this year the focal point of the adoption area is going to be Chance. It'll be perfect for the community to meet him."

Chance would be the focus? Pride at being able to show him off to the public surged through Aaron. When pain at the thought of losing him tried to worm its way into the pride, he shoved it down and swallowed hard.

"Has anyone come in to look at him yet?"

Maria sighed and shook her head. "No…not even one inquiry. That's a little unusual, even for a pit bull. By now we should have had someone ask about him. It's not uncommon for dogs to be here for a while, especially his breed, but usually there are at least inquires. Don't worry, though. We'll get him a home. Every day that passes is just one day closer to the right one. Remember that. He's a special dog and will get a special home. We just need to find the family that will see past his exterior."

Despite her enthusiasm, Aaron didn't feel so sure. He was worried. Chance was a special dog and no one wanted to look at him. Why, he wondered? What was the reason? He was still a fairly young dog, so that would make him appealing to families that wanted a pet to stay with them a long time.

It boggled his mind.

As the day came, decorations and posters went up around the shelter—more so than usual. Even Sandra decorated the large front desk and made it pet friendly. Though everything was always kept as clean as possible, even more volunteers showed up the night before to scrub the place down again. All blankets and towels were washed—even if they were already clean—and the animals were given baths.

Aaron paid special attention to Chance, making sure his short fur shone in the light. He couldn't do anything for the scars, but he brought in a new collar he had purchased especially for him. As soon as his bath was over and the dog had been dried, he attached it.

"Looking handsome, buddy."

Chance licked his face and tried to crawl into his lap. Aaron laughed and pushed him off. He snuck an extra blanket into his kennel and fluffed up his bed for him. Chance ruined it quickly when he climbed onto the small cot, turned a few times, dug into the blankets, and disheveled them. He settled down with a yawn as if his life exhausted him. Aaron placed his favorite rope toy next to him on the cot.

"Tomorrow you're going to a great home. I can feel it," he said, hoping his optimism would make his wish come true. Chance just looked at him with his head cocked to the side, one ear tilted appealingly.

The next day, Aaron woke up earlier than usual to get ready for a long day at the shelter. He dug through his closet and dresser, looking for something to wear. He wanted to look good, but he knew he had to be comfortable, too. In the end he chose a darker pair of jeans and a black T-shirt.

The fundraising event started at ten and ran until five, and Aaron got there at eight to help set up. All of the available volunteers were on hand to help with the event, and Maria directed them to put together the final touches.

Senior staff would handle the cash donations and adoption paperwork. Volunteers would show visitors to the animals and handle the item donations. One storage room had been cleaned out and waited to hold everything until it could be sorted later that weekend. Aaron knew he and Finn would be put on that duty.

Just before ten, the first people arrived. Aaron's body filled with a nervous energy; every person he saw walk through that door was a potential family for Chance. Maria practically jumped on the first family that had come in. Not only did they donate a considerable amount of money, they also wanted to adopt a few dogs. She took them to the back personally. Another family came in a little while after them. The children with them bounced around in excitement and exclaimed over looking at the puppies.

"Actually," the mother said, "we're looking to adopt a dog that's a little older. We want one that's already trained."

"I can show you the dogs," Aaron said, stepping in excitedly. "Welcome to Happy Endings Animal Foundation," he said as he led them toward the dogs. "All of our dogs are spayed or neutered before they're adopted out, and all are up to date on shots," he added, as he had been instructed. "Is there a particular breed or quality you were looking for?" Aaron asked, hoping they would say no.

The husband shook his head as Aaron walked backward, leading them down the aisle. The children could hardly be contained in their enthusiasm as they passed each cage. "We are hoping for a dog that's good with kids and other animals. We have a cat at home as well and a large backyard. My wife loves lap dogs, but I don't."

"I've agreed that maybe a larger dog would be best for the children. Less likely that they would hurt it," the woman added.

"Great! I have the perfect dog for you," Aaron said, leading them directly to the end. "Chance is trained in basic obedience and commands, and he loves cats. He's a great dog with children, full of energy, and he's about three years old."

He stopped them at the last kennel where Chance sat, happily wagging his tail. His tongue lolled out of his mouth, and with his new collar he looked fantastic. Attached to a poster board outside his kennel were pictures of him and the volunteers and other shots Maria had gotten from the website.

The kids seemed happy with the dog and called to him, but the man looked skeptically at his wife, then at Aaron, who had crouched down with the kids and handed Chance a treat through the chain-link gate.

"What breed is he?"

"He's an American pit bull terrier. One of the best family breeds out there," Aaron said and pointed out the history of the breed that was attached to the board, as well. He personally had made sure that it had been included to further entice people…and at the very least, educate them.

"I should have been specific. We're not looking for a certain breed, but we don't want any of the bully breeds."

"There's too much risk," the woman added, though she remained crouched at her children's sides.

Aaron opened his mouth to argue with them, to tell them there was a risk with *any* dog, but remembered what had happened before. He closed his mouth with a quick snap, smiled as sweetly as he could and nodded. "Well, in that case there are plenty of other dogs that should be appealing." *It's okay,* he told himself. *It's only half past ten. There's still plenty of time to find Chance a home. This is only the first family. One step closer, like Maria said.*

As the day wore on, Aaron helped families find cats and one other family find a dog. He also took in a lot of food and used-towel donations. When he asked Savannah about them, she explained that used towels were perfect to donate. They cost nothing for the families except for the replacements, they didn't add to landfills, and the animals didn't know the difference.

"They're great because if they get ruined right away, we don't have to feel bad about getting rid of them. And when the towels get holes in them, we just cut them up and use them as cleaning rags. Every little thing is used over and over until it literally falls apart," she added with a laugh.

It made sense to Aaron, and he enthusiastically helped every family that dropped off supplies. Most didn't even come into the shelter, even at the coaxing of the volunteers. The drop-off tent that Finn had the mind to set up collected piles of items, and Aaron helped carry them inside when he wasn't busy with people. The room began to fill with food, toys, and other desperately needed items.

At four, Aaron went to check on Chance. When he asked other volunteers how it was going, they gave him a sad smile and shook their heads.

"Hang in there," Finn said, slapping him on the back. "There's still an hour left."

Aaron sighed and crouched down in front of Chance's kennel. Even Chance—the dog he'd grown so attached to—looked defeated. He lay on his bed, as if he knew what was happening around him and how the adopters felt when they saw him. When he saw Aaron, though, his head perked up a little and his tail wagged slowly.

"Hey, buddy. How you hanging in there?" he asked, wondering what Chance would say if he could actually respond. "I have to get back to work, but when this is all over I'll come and visit you," he promised.

As the last hour wound down, fewer people came by, and then no one. The silence hung thickly around everyone as they broke down the tent and the signs outside.

Maria sat in her office, pleased, as she and Amy added the totals together. "We did well this year," she announced as Aaron poked his head in. "The food donated should last us a few weeks, and we raised a couple thousand dollars. That's huge!"

"How many adoption applications were put in?"

"We had five dog applications put in and fourteen cats. Some siblings were put in for together. It's not as big as we've had in the past, but with the economy the way it is, that's understandable. Still, we did very well today. Tomorrow I'll put the calls out and see if I can get these animals placed as soon as possible to give us some room."

"One of them…would Chance be one of those dogs?"

Amy quickly glanced at her paperwork and Maria shook her head sadly. "I'm sorry, Aaron. But don't give up. There were a lot of dogs that didn't get placed today. He's not the only one."

Aaron nodded and said good-bye to both of them. "I'll see you tomorrow."

"Yes, tomorrow. Thank you for all of your hard work today!" Maria called after him.

Finn was busy so Aaron didn't bother finding him to say good-bye. Besides, he wasn't in the mood for light conversation. Instead he spent a few minutes with Chance before he said good night, gave him a special treat, and then snuck out the back and around to the front to avoid the others.

Chance wasn't one of the dogs who found a home. Aaron turned down a side street, dreading the thought of going home and facing Mom. At a light, he leaned against the steering wheel, trying to press the hollow sensation out of his chest. So many people had been in to see the animals. How could it be that not a single person wanted to take Chance home? Weren't there some sort of odds that would be in the dog's favor?

By the time Aaron pulled into the driveway he'd made up his mind to avoid his mother at all costs. Not only were his eyes red and just a little bit puffy, but she would be cheerful and he wanted to sulk for as long as possible. Maybe it was selfish, but he had been wishing so hard. *It's all I wanted out of today. I just want Chance to find a good home. Why can't people see how great he is?*

Trying to sneak into the house as quietly as possible, Aaron made his way upstairs to his room and grabbed clean clothes. He smelled like all the different animals at the shelter and desperately needed a shower. Besides, it would keep him away from his mother even longer.

"Aaron, is that you? I didn't hear you come in," his mother called up the stairs. Pretending he didn't hear her, he shut the bathroom door behind him and turned the shower on quickly. Making it as hot as he could stand, he stripped down and jumped in.

The heated water soothed muscles he didn't even know were aching. He stood there a long time, letting the water wash over him before he grabbed his shampoo and started scrubbing his hair. Soon the steam clouded the bathroom and made it hard to see. By the time he finished and stepped out of the shower, the bathroom mirror had fogged over completely and mist filled the room.

Using his towel, he wiped a streak off the mirror and stared at his reflection. Looking back at him was a young man with red hair and green eyes. A smattering of freckles dusted his cheeks and nose. While he had fair skin to begin with, the scars were even paler. The corner of his mouth turned down, even when he tried to smile at himself. But despite the twisted appearance, he no longer found himself ugly. The person he had been at the beginning of his journey was different from the person who stood in front of the mirror. He smiled at the scarred reflection and pushed his hair out of his eyes. If he could change the way he saw himself, then surely someone would see the same in Chance, a defenseless animal.

And now that he saw beyond his own scars, maybe he'd find a guy who could see past them, as well. Someone who wasn't straight like Finn. Someone he'd be able to call his boyfriend. His *first* boyfriend. He might be sixteen, and he might be a little late to the game, unlike his friends, but there had to be someone out there for him, right?

A knock on the door startled him from his thoughts, and even though he had locked the door, he whipped the towel around his hips.

"What?" he snapped.

"Are you okay?" his mother called through the door.

"Yeah, I'm fine. Just needed a shower. I'll be down in a few minutes."

"Okay. Dinner is on the table. Don't take too long or it'll get cold."

Aaron dried off and dressed in his clean clothes. When he opened the door, he could hear his mother downstairs in the kitchen. He found her seated at the table, nearly finished with her food.

"Sorry," he said as he sat down. "I smelled from the shelter."

"How did it go today?"

He related the successes they'd had and told her about all of the supplies they had taken in. When he mentioned that Chance hadn't been adopted, she frowned.

"I know how much you were hoping he would find a home."

"It's okay. He'll find a good home soon. I'm sure of it. I wish we could adopt him, though," he mentioned, finally voicing the idea that had taken root in his mind and steadily grown over the last few weeks.

"Aaron…I know you'd like to, and I've thought of it myself, but you know we can't."

"I know," he said, though it surprised him that his mother had the same idea.

"It was one thing with the kitten and your father paying the vet bills, but a dog is so much more. It's another type of food, it's a lot of time and effort, and the bills would be even higher. Even your father can't afford that, and it would be unfair to ask him."

"I know, Mom," he repeated. "It's okay. I understand." Sighing, he stood up.

"Aaron?"

"Sorry," he said as he picked up his plate of mostly untouched food. "Just not that hungry."

"But—"

He carried the plate to the kitchen, dumped it in a container, and placed it in the fridge. When Mom followed him and tried to get him to talk, he brushed her off and dashed up the steps.

He'd told her he understood, but maybe he didn't.

CHAPTER SEVENTEEN

I'd like you to meet her," his father said over the phone. Aaron had been surprised at the call and even more so by the subject of it. "Rebecca has been asking about you, and things are going very well with her."

"Um, okay," Aaron said, not sure how to take it, what to say. "That would be cool, I guess."

His father breathed a sigh of relief. "Great. Excellent. How about tomorrow night? We'll go somewhere casual, so don't dress up or anything."

Aaron nodded and realized his father couldn't see him. "Okay, that's cool, Dad. Where should I meet you?"

"No, no. We'll pick you up at five."

Great, so he would have to endure an awkward car ride there.

"Okay, see you tomorrow then, Dad."

He hung up the phone and flopped backward on his bed.

His mother knocked on the door frame and poked her head inside. "What did he have to say?"

"He wants to go out for dinner tomorrow night so I can meet Rebecca. What do you think of this, Mom?"

"Your father knows what he's doing. It's none of my business."

Aaron frowned at her and tossed her the phone, which she caught with one hand. "How come you haven't gone on dates?"

She raised one delicate eyebrow and stared at him. "I could ask you the same."

"Mom!" Aaron felt himself turn red. "It's not the same!"

"Well, you *can* go on dates, you know."

"I thought moms weren't supposed to say that."

"No, moms are supposed to say things like *No sex* or *If you have sex, make sure you use protection.* But I know I raised you well, and you're a smart boy."

Aaron's entire neck burned with embarrassment and his mother laughed as she left the room.

❖

His father picked him up promptly at five the next night. He came inside and greeted Aaron's mother for a moment before the two of them turned and left. "I picked her up first so you wouldn't have to wait in the car."

"But now she's had to wait in the car."

"She assured me she doesn't mind."

Aaron felt awkward as he climbed into the back, and he wished his father had let him drive over there to meet them.

The woman in the front seat was a pretty brunette, and her hair was pulled back and put in a clip. In the dim light afforded by the car when his father opened his door, he saw a few streaks of gray running through her dark hair. She turned to smile at him and he noticed thick square-framed glasses.

"Hello, Aaron. It's a pleasure to meet you," she said softly. She reached over the back of the seat, holding out her hand. It was an awkward position for her, so Aaron reached forward and took her hand.

"Likewise."

She must have smiled a lot because little crow's feet wrinkled by her eyes when her lips quirked up. "Your father has told me so much about you, but I hope you'll fill in what he missed at dinner."

"Sure," he said, uncertain how else he could respond.

Dad drummed on the steering wheel as he drove, and the three of them lapsed into an awkward silence. Ten minutes into the drive, Rebecca and his father started to talk. With him in the backseat and the radio on, it was difficult to understand what they were saying unless Rebecca turned and directed a question at him. Mostly he just smiled and nodded, agreeing with whatever they said.

Aaron was happy to see that they were going to be comfortable at Grayson's, a well-known restaurant in town, decorated with homey wood paneling and an assortment of pictures and memorabilia from different eras the restaurant had seen. The dinner crowd hadn't hit that place for the night, so they had no trouble getting seated at a booth. Rebecca slid in first, with his father next to her, so Aaron took the bench across from them. At least he had room to stretch out.

"So," Rebecca started when the waiter brought them all glasses of water. "Your father said you're volunteering at an animal shelter this summer. How do you like it?" she asked, her eyes flicking to the scars across his face.

"I enjoy it. It's a lot of work, and there's always something that needs to be done, but it's fun. I made a lot of friends and I've met some great animals."

"Aaron's also been able to conquer his fear of dogs," Dad said proudly.

"Dad."

"Sorry, son." Dad beamed, and Aaron rolled his eyes.

They took some time to view the menu before the waitress came back and took their order. As usual, Aaron ordered a cheeseburger and fries.

"So…you're a sophomore in school?" Rebecca asked once the waitress left with their order.

"Yes. At least I was. I'll be a junior in the fall," Aaron replied and then turned the questions around on her. "What do you do for work? Dad said you met when he was showing a house."

"I work at a bank," she said. "It's a good job, and I enjoy the people I work with."

"Do you have any pets?"

"I do. I have a Ragdoll cat."

"Oh…those are beautiful. We had one in at the shelter, but it was adopted at the fundraiser we had."

"I'm surprised one even made it to a shelter. They're such wonderful cats. Very highly sought after."

Aaron agreed. "She was the first one to go, and she hadn't been there very long."

"Do you have a part-time job besides your shelter work, too?"

"No, not yet," Aaron said. "I do want to get one, though, and I put in a few applications around town. I'm hoping my friend, Finn, from the shelter, can get me in at the bookstore he works at."

Rebecca smiled at him. "Well, you sound like a very busy young man. Your mother must be very proud of you. I know your father brags all the time."

Aaron shrugged.

The conversation lagged for a few minutes, and his father started to speak with Rebecca to fill in the gap. The silence didn't feel as comfortable as the lapses in conversation he had with his friends. When the waiter brought their food, it gave Aaron even more time to keep to himself. He ate his burger more slowly than he normally would, but after a few bites, Rebecca tossed more questions at him.

"You're so busy with volunteer work and possibly a job soon. Will you get to see your friends very often?"

"I usually work the same shift as Finn at the shelter, and my other friends stop by when they know I'm at home. So yeah, I get to see them often enough. And when Finn is working at the bookstore I'll drop by and see him."

"Do you have time for a girlfriend?"

Aaron glanced at his father and raised an eyebrow. His father shook his head and discreetly gestured toward him. No, he hadn't told her. That was Aaron's business and his to tell if he wanted to. While he appreciated it, he hoped it didn't make the rest of the night awkward.

"No time for a girlfriend." Rebecca started to say something about it being a shame, but Aaron interrupted. "But maybe I'll have time for a boyfriend."

Rebecca stopped, her mouth open for a moment before she closed it and turned to look at his father bemusedly. His father just shrugged and took a bite of his pasta, chewing thoughtfully. She looked back at Aaron; he stared at her as pointedly as he could.

"Oh. Well…in that case…" she started but didn't seem to know what to say.

"Aaron came out to us when he was, what? Twelve? Thirteen? It was so long ago I don't even remember." His father laughed.

"It wasn't that long ago, Dad. You must be getting old. If your memory is slipping that much maybe you need to be checked for Alzheimer's."

His father laughed and soon Rebecca joined in awkwardly.

Aaron could see she hadn't expected that answer and didn't know how to take it. Should he push it further? See what she made of it? *Will Dad continue dating her if she has a problem with me being gay?*

The rest of the dinner felt stiff. Aaron couldn't loosen up and join the conversation with Rebecca and his father as much as he wanted to. She seemed like a nice, funny woman who could laugh at herself when the occasion called for it, but if she had a problem with him being gay, it would stunt their relationship.

When the evening had clearly ended and their meal had been paid for, the three piled into the car, and his father turned toward Aaron's home.

"It was...great getting to know you, Aaron." There was a hesitation in her voice that bothered Aaron.

"Same here, Rebecca," he said. He wanted to ask if she really meant it but kept his mouth shut.

"I hope we can do this again, soon. Maybe spend a day together next time? Get to know you even better?"

Aaron smiled from his seat and looked out the window at the passing buildings. The sun faded in the sky but it was still bright out, and he enjoyed the ride, despite the earlier tension. "Yeah, I think that would be okay."

His father dropped him off, and he waved to the two of them before dashing into the house. "I'm home, Mom!" he called. Mom sat in the living room watching a movie with a bowl of popcorn.

"How was dinner?"

"Eh, it was okay," he said as he sat down and joined her. She had on *The Mummy*, one of her favorites.

"Did you like Rebecca?"

Aaron hesitated, unsure of how he should answer. Would he be betraying his mother if he said that she seemed okay, aside from one possible problem? She answered that question for him.

"It's okay if you like her, you know."

He breathed a sigh of relief. "She's okay. She's kind of funny, but…"

"But?" she asked.

"Dad didn't tell her I'm gay, and she didn't seem to know how to react to that."

She patted his leg and offered him the bowl of popcorn. "Well, she'll have to learn to accept it. It's part of who you are. Your father might like her, but she'd better not cause any problems for you." She left it at that and then smiled at him. "Watch the movie with me?"

"Of course," he said and settled in to spend the night with his mom.

CHAPTER EIGHTEEN

Aaron finally found a job. It wasn't much, just fifteen to twenty hours a week, but it would give him a little bit of cash to spend, and it would help his mother out with the gas money she gave him for the car. It also left him plenty of time to volunteer at the shelter, too.

As the summer crept on and June gave way to July, Aaron found himself saving his money and working hard at the shelter. He snuck in gifts to Chance every so often—just a new toy or something—and tried to show him off to every person or family looking to adopt. He grew increasingly frustrated, though, as each person looked at Chance with mild disgust and turned to one of the other dogs.

Chance had already been at the shelter for over two and a half months, and Aaron worried. Every other dog that had been there when Chance arrived had been adopted out, and even some of the second batch had come and gone, as well. Maria had posted Chance's photos and story on a pet finder website to help people from all over the country locate him. While there had been some hits and a few inquiries made, no one called to say they were interested.

Was there something wrong with the information or the pictures? Did the database not work right? Could people not see Chance's information?

Worry started to cloud Aaron's mind, so one day he walked in for his shift and went directly to Maria's office. She sat at her desk looking at paperwork when he knocked.

"Oh, good morning, Aaron. What can I do for you?"

"Maria, it's about Chance."

She nodded and gestured for him to take a seat. "What's on your mind?"

"How long do you keep dogs here? I mean is there a certain time frame for a dog that's staying here?"

Maria frowned and looked up at him. She put her pen down and folded her hands. "We've never had that issue. All dogs get adopted."

"But…what if there's one dog that couldn't be adopted? What would happen? Would they go to another shelter? Or a sanctuary?"

"All of our animals are linked to a national network so people all over the country can look at them. The possibilities of Chance not finding a home are very slim. It just might take some time."

"But how much time? I need to know—how much time does Chance have before it runs out? I know how much it costs to keep an animal here. You can't keep him here indefinitely, can you? And that's not a good life for him, being cooped up in a kennel for hours a day."

Maria ran her hand across her forehead and sighed. "Aaron…" She paused and looked at him straight. "No, you're right. We can't keep an animal here indefinitely. We just don't have the means. And while we strive to be a no-kill shelter rather than a limited euthanasia shelter, there are some instances where even no-kills have to make an exception if it's in the best interest of the dog."

"But Chance's best interest is being in a home!"

"I agree. If we can find him one. But if we can't…I'm afraid there aren't very many options."

"Don't you have a foster who could take him in? Couldn't you?"

"I'm sorry. I have too many animals at home, as it is. If he were a smaller dog, yes, I would, but he's very high energy, and I'm not home as much as he would need me to be."

"What about Amy?"

"She's already fostered so many of our animals. I've asked her about Chance, but she can't take him. None of our regular fosters can. They're just overwhelmed, at the moment."

Aaron thought quickly. "What about other shelters? Surely there's some sort of network of fosters out there, or a sanctuary he could go to and—"

"Aaron. I assure you. Everything I can do, I have done. We will keep trying until we can't anymore."

But it was the *can't anymore* that terrified him.

With nothing left to say, he stood and left the office. How could they have done everything? Wouldn't a sanctuary take him right away? Or a facility that trained therapy animals? He would qualify for that. Aaron had worked with him, and so had the senior staff. They all said he would be great! Maybe if he made some calls himself, they would see how passionately he felt and someone would step in before it was too late.

Finn found him an hour later with Chance curled up on his lap out in the sun, taking a nap. Aaron stroked his fur absentmindedly while he thought of different ideas, anything to save this sweet dog.

"Hey. What's up? I haven't seen you around."

"I've been out here."

"Clearly. And you didn't put on sunblock, either, because your skin is bright red."

Aaron reached up and touched his face, and Finn grimaced. "Dude, you need to put something on that. When you pulled your fingers away your skin was white. That's not good."

"I burn easily."

"Yeah, well, all the more reason to put sunblock on. What's going on?"

"I keep trying to be positive about someone adopting Chance, but it's not looking good."

"What do you mean?"

Shifting a bit to get out of the sun, Aaron relayed what Maria had told him. When he finished, Finn was deep in thought.

"If I didn't live in an apartment or have such assholes for parents, I would adopt him myself," Finn said. "But as much as I want to, there's no way."

"I know that. And I wish I could take him home, but Mom really can't afford it. I've got some money saved, but it's not enough to take care of him."

"What if you contact the animal control officer who brought him to us? Maybe he'd be interested. I'm sure Maria has the contact information somewhere in her office. Or if you can just find out his name, you could find him yourself."

Aaron perked up. "You think that might work?"

Finn shrugged. "Don't know, but it couldn't hurt to try, could it? At this point, what do you have to lose?"

❖

In the end, Aaron wasn't able to get the information from Maria's office; he worried too much about being caught where he shouldn't be. Finn, however, didn't worry about that. He told Aaron he'd done it plenty of times. When Maria left to take her lunch, Finn casually strode into her office and started searching through her paperwork.

Three large filing cabinets stood against one wall, holding all of the paperwork for the animals the shelter had taken in over the years. Because Finn didn't know Chance's number off the top of his head, he had a hard time finding it, but he finally did. He jotted down the name of the officer and scooted out of the office before Maria returned.

"Got it," he announced to Aaron when he found him playing with Gloria, a German shepherd mix. "You want to call Officer James Hardy."

"Excellent. I owe you." Aaron grinned. He ruffled Gloria's fur and took the name and number from Finn. "I'm going on break. I'll call him right now."

"Good luck," Finn called after him.

Aaron grabbed his cell phone out of the staff room and took it outside, where it would be quieter. He grabbed a Coke and told Sandra on the way out that he was taking ten minutes. She nodded and waved him off.

He expected to reach Officer Hardy on the first try, but when he got through to the department Aaron learned that he was out in the field and wasn't due back until six. He frowned but left a message with the man who answered.

"Can you have him call Aaron Cassidy?" He gave him his cell phone number and a brief description about why he called. "Please tell him it's urgent."

Though the officer sounded skeptical, he accepted the information. Discouragement nipped at Aaron's heels, but he wouldn't give up.

When he found Finn after his break was up, his friend asked him how it went.

"Officer Hardy is in the field and won't be off until my shift is over."

"Did you expect to get in touch with him right away? It might take a little time, Aaron. He's a busy man, I'm sure."

"I guess I did expect to get hold of him the first time."

"You're an idealist. Not that it's bad, but not everything works out the way we want."

Aaron shrugged his agreement and got back to work.

"Have you heard from your dad?"

Come to think of it… "Not since the dinner with his girlfriend, actually. It's not like him not to call once in a while and check in. But I haven't called either, I guess."

Finn shrugged. "Maybe you should call."

"Don't know what I'd say," Aaron admitted.

At five, his shift was over and he muttered good-byes to everyone else and left. He kept his cell phone in his lap on the drive home, kept it on the bathroom counter while he showered, and left it out on the table while he ate dinner, much to his mother's dismay.

By six thirty, Officer Hardy still hadn't returned his call, and he knew his disappointment showed.

"What's going on?" Mom asked, resting her chin on her hand. "You keep staring at your phone. Are you waiting on a call from a boy?" she asked with a sly smile.

"No, I'm worried about Chance," he said, not rising to her bait and then told her what Maria had talked about today. The smile slipped from her face. "I'm waiting for Officer Hardy to call. Finn and I thought maybe he could help."

His mother glanced at the table and tilted her head to the side. "How do you think he would be able to help?"

"Well, I thought…" Aaron started, then got up and started pacing. "I've read so much about pit bulls used as therapy dogs or even in law enforcement. Maybe Chance could be trained for that. And since we can't find anyone else to adopt him, maybe the man who found him in the first place will take an interest in helping him out. I don't think he'd like to know a dog he helped save might be destroyed." Sharp pain stabbed through Aaron's chest at voicing that one word.

His blood ran cold and the food he'd just eaten quickly unsettled. He'd never let it happen. He couldn't.

Tapping her chin, she nodded. "Yes, that could be. I guess it is worth a shot."

The two finished their dinner, though Aaron had little appetite left, and like always, he helped his mother clean up. He loaded the dishes in the dishwasher while she wiped down the table. Rather than moving to the television like they normally did, his mother grabbed two glasses of iced tea and brought them outside.

Most of the time they sat silently, sipping their drinks and watching the birds in the yard. Midnight mewed from time to time at the screen door, but they ignored him. At eight, Aaron started when his cell phone rang. Without glancing at the number he answered.

"Hello?"

"Hello, I'm looking for Aaron Cassidy," a deep voice said.

"This is Aaron."

"Aaron, this is Officer Hardy. I received a message to call you, that it was urgent. What can I do for you?"

Aaron's heart leapt into his throat and he stood, moving to the other side of the small patio. Mom watched him intently.

"Mister—uh, Officer Hardy. Thank you so much for returning my call. I understand that you're busy, but I hoped that maybe you would have some time to talk. Do you remember the dog you brought to the Happy Endings Animal Foundation about three months ago?"

The man chuckled faintly. "Of course I remember. A scarred pit bull, correct?"

"Yes, that's Chance."

"Ah, so he has a name now. Great name. How is Chance doing?"

"He's doing very well, sir," Aaron explained excitedly, going into detail about the wonderful progress he had made and how sweet he was when it came to people and other animals.

"That's fantastic to hear. I thank you for the update. To be honest I'd meant to check in with the director, but things come up, as I'm sure you know."

"Yes, but I didn't just call to update you. You see, I kind of hoped you'd be able to help me—us—out."

Officer Hardy paused. "Help you out? How so?"

Aaron took a deep breath and, for what felt like the fiftieth time, told him what the shelter faced with Chance: how they had tried to find a family but couldn't, how his time seemed to be running out.

Another long pause filled the line and Aaron thought maybe his phone had dropped the call. He pulled back to glance at the screen and saw that not only did he have full reception, he was still connected.

"Officer Hardy?" he finally asked.

"I'm here, sorry kid. Just thinking. I'm not sure how I can help you out, but I'll do my best. I'll put in a good word around here. Tomorrow before my shift, I'll stop by to take a look at the dog for myself. Maybe we can work something out."

"Do you think maybe you'd be interested in adopting him?" he asked hopefully.

"No can do. My wife and son are allergic to dogs. If it wasn't for that, I might be interested, though. But I'll ask around."

Aaron's heart sank, but he agreed to meet him tomorrow at the shelter. When he hung up the phone, his lips pulled down in a frown.

"I'm sorry it didn't go the way you'd hoped," his mother said softly from her seat. She hadn't moved the entire time they were on the phone.

"I never thought it would be this hard," he said as he joined her in the seat he had vacated earlier.

"No matter what happens, Aaron, be proud of yourself. I'm proud of you. You've gone through so much in the last few months, and you've overcome your fears. Not only that, but you've fought for an animal you would have, at one time, run away from. That's not something to be taken lightly."

Aaron nodded. "I know it's not, but I still feel like I'm not doing enough."

"Nothing ever feels like it's enough, but sometimes...well, sometimes we have to accept that it is. But I don't expect you to give up until the very end. You're a fighter. And so is Chance."

At his mother's words, a single thought started to form in his mind. Although his mother had told him no before to adopting Chance, a plan suddenly hatched and his face brightened. When his mother looked at him, he shrugged it off, gulped down his iced tea, kissed her cheek, and explained that he had some research to do. Without another word he dashed up the stairs to his room.

His father had offered to pay the vet bills for Little Dipper. Chance was a healthy dog whose initial shots and neutering had been taken care of by the shelter. An enormous expense had been taken care of, already. So aside from food, a yearly checkup should be all he needed. If he could convince his father to pay the same amount he would have paid for Little Dipper, perhaps with his part-time job he would have enough to cover the rest of the expenses. Why hadn't he thought of it before?

Of course, that factored in him keeping the job he had now. He had saved most of the money so far, aside from gas expenses and going out with Angelo, Miguel, and Vicki for dinner once. He would have to work extra hard at his job to convince them to keep him once summer ended. He would also have to convince his mother to let him work during the school year. And it might mean cutting down time at the shelter to just Saturdays and Sundays during the school year to keep his job and his grades up. But if it meant he could adopt Chance, he would do it.

CHAPTER NINETEEN

Officer Hardy showed up exactly when he said he would the next morning, and Aaron greeted him with a smile. He had done his research the night before and if he kept his job, he would be able to adopt Chance—as long as no outrageous illnesses or injuries popped up. But he wouldn't stop looking for Chance's forever home in the meantime. The officer shook his hand, and Aaron led him to view the dogs.

Chance lay on his bed, gnawing on a rawhide bone when they approached, and he perked up when Aaron stopped in front of his kennel.

"This is Chance."

Hardy knelt in front of the gate and let the dog lick his fingers. "Wow, he looks like a completely different dog. You all have done remarkable work with him," he exclaimed, chuckling as Chance rubbed his side against the gate. "To be honest, when we found him, I thought for sure he was a hopeless case. Most times, any animals that have clearly been used in dogfights are put down. But he seems like a totally different creature."

"He is. He's gotten to know all the staff and he's very affectionate. He loves kittens and he plays well with other dogs, too."

"Incredible. I commend the entire staff here."

Aaron clasped his hands behind his back and rocked back on his heels. "So…do you think maybe you could help us find him a home?"

"There are some people who might be interested at the station. I'll let them know, but I can't promise anything."

With a grin on his face, Aaron thanked him and led him out of the dog kennels. He watched as Officer Hardy got into his car and took off for the station.

With renewed hope, sure that either someone at the station would adopt Chance or he'd convince his parents of his ability to care for the dog, Aaron threw himself into his work. After he got out, he would call his father and propose the idea to him first. If Dad agreed, he would just have to convince his mother. He couldn't tackle her first, because she would tell him to leave his father alone.

When Finn came in, he told him of his plans and of Officer Hardy stopping by. Finn thought it was a great idea and offered to help him find a vet that would help Aaron and Chance. He also offered to try and help him convince his parents, if necessary.

"When are you going to ask?"

"Probably tonight. Or at least call and see if I can go out with Dad and tell him in person what I'd like to do."

"Do you think he'll go for it?" Finn asked as he stooped down to grab a bundle of blankets that needed to be washed.

"I don't know. I think so. I mean, he wanted to help pay for the kitten. Remember that? It might take some convincing, but it'll work out."

That night after Aaron got home, he sat on his bed and dialed his father's number. For the first time in weeks his father actually picked up the first time he called. He had gotten so used to him being out with Rebecca that it startled him when he heard his actual voice rather than the recording.

"Oh, hi, Dad. What's up?"

"Not much, how are you, kiddo? I wasn't expecting your call. Is everything okay?"

"Yeah, everything's cool. I wanted to see if maybe you'd want to go out to dinner or something soon. I need to talk to you."

"Need to talk to me, huh? Sure, we can do that. How does tomorrow night sound?"

"Sounds good. Thanks, Dad. How is everything going with Rebecca?"

"Things are going well. I'll update you on everything when we go out."

"Okay. Does Gracie's sound good?"

"Sure. I'll meet you there after work."

"And Dad? You can...bring Rebecca if you want."

There was a pause on the line, and then Dad replied, "I'll ask her."

❖

Aaron had to work the next day, so he didn't get to see Chance, but plenty of customers helped him stay busy. By the time he got off his shift at the clothing store, his stomach growled and he couldn't wait to eat. He didn't have time to go home and change, so he went directly to the restaurant and claimed a booth for him and his dad inside. He waited anxiously, wondering if Rebecca would come, as well.

He waited over twenty minutes and was about to send his dad a text asking where he was when he walked in the front door. He saw Aaron sitting in a booth, almost finished with his first glass of Coke, and approached.

"I'm sorry, Aaron. I got stuck at a house later than I thought. Did you order yet?"

Aaron shook his head. "No, I was waiting for you. Rebecca didn't come?"

"She...was busy. Let's order and then we'll talk," he said as he waved the waitress over. Both ordered burgers and the waitress disappeared to refill Aaron's Coke and get his father water.

"So what's going on? You sounded pretty impatient on the phone yesterday."

"Did I?" Aaron asked, tilting his head to the side. He hadn't realized it. "Eager, I guess. A lot has been going on at the shelter, and I wanted to talk to you about it."

"How's Chance?"

"Well, that's the thing, Dad. Maria can't find someone to adopt him. I'm afraid he...his time might be running out."

"I thought it was a no-kill shelter."

"It tries to be, but it's actually limited euthanasia," Aaron said and explained what Maria had told him. "Pretty much the last chance for him is someone at the police department, or…" Aaron stopped and looked at his father.

"Or what?"

Aaron glared at the waitress when she interrupted them to tell them the food would be out in a few minutes. She left, and he turned back to his father.

"Dad, remember how you offered to pay for the kitten I wanted? But when we got to the shelter the next day, he had already been adopted?"

His father looked at him with narrowed, curious eyes and nodded. "Yes, I remember that. You were upset."

"Right. I never found another animal I liked as much as that kitten. Until now."

"Now? You mean…you want to adopt Chance?"

"Yes! Please, Dad? I know he's expensive, but—"

"He is expensive, Aaron. I wouldn't be able to foot that much of a vet bill."

Aaron let out a frustrated sigh. "Please let me finish. I have an idea. What if you pay just the amount you were willing to pay for me to get Little Dipper? I can pay for the rest."

"You?" His father sat back and stared at him. "How are you going to afford that dog?"

"With my job. I've been saving my money, and I have quite a bit put away. I have a plan and I think it will work. See, if I can keep my job throughout the school year, I'll be able to afford him."

"Shouldn't you be saving for college? And what if you *can't* keep your job?"

"Dad, please. This is something I really want to do. It's not like I'm asking for just any dog. I'm asking to rescue a dog and give him a good life. Haven't you always told me to do the right thing?" He paused, let that sink in. "This *is* the right thing, Dad. I know it is."

His father hesitated and waited as the waitress delivered their burgers. He took a slow bite and then ate a few fries while Aaron sat on pins and needles waiting. "What does your mother say about all this?"

Sheepishly, Aaron glanced down at his plate and picked at his fries, pushing them around the rim. He dipped a few in ketchup, swirled them around and chomped down on them. "I didn't ask her yet. I figured if I had your permission first, and your assistance, I would get a better reaction from her. She would say no just like she did with Little Dipper until you offered to help."

Grunting his agreement, Dad wiped his mouth with a napkin. "I suppose you're right on that account. Do you know how much it costs to raise a dog? I don't mean just money, but time?"

"I've been working at the shelter for a few months now, Dad. I'm pretty sure I have a good idea."

"Well, I guess you would know better than anyone else." He smiled. "I can't offer much more than I could with the kitten, but if your mother agrees…as long as she doesn't try to kill me for offering."

Aaron nearly exploded out of his seat, cheering. Other patrons of the restaurant turned to glance at them. He glanced down in embarrassment. So much for staying calm. "Can we talk to her right after this? Please? Pretty please?"

His father laughed loudly. "What are you, five again?" He sighed exaggeratedly. "I suppose we could. But don't rush through your food just to get home and talk to her. You'll make yourself sick."

"Okay, sorry," he said, but he couldn't fight the grin that took over his face. It was so big it even lifted the scarred corner of his mouth.

The two ate in silence for a few moments before Aaron remembered Rebecca. In his excitement over his father's agreement, she'd completely slipped from his thoughts.

"So what about Rebecca? Why didn't she come? Did she have to work?" Dad looked up at him and took a sip of his drink. When he hesitated Aaron looked down at his food. "She's got a problem with my being gay, doesn't she?"

"She doesn't have a problem with it, son. It's just…not what she expected."

"So?"

"It'll take some getting used to for her. That's all."

"What is there to get used to?"

"Just give her some time."

"Dad, what if I give her time and she doesn't get used to it? What if she can't handle it? Are you going to stop coming around and spend more time with her?"

Jerking his head up, Dad looked at him, stunned. "Aaron! I can't believe you'd even suggest something like that. Of course I wouldn't stop our visits. That has nothing to do with Rebecca."

"Doesn't it, though? You're dating her."

"Son." Dad pushed his food out of the way and leaned on the table. His usually cheerful face had been replaced by a serious mask. "You are my son. Yes, I like Rebecca, and she's someone I care about and could spend a long time with. But you come first. I support you completely. I thought you knew that, but maybe I haven't been so good at showing it lately."

"No, Dad, you have. I just…I worried. I mean, I've heard things, but I should have known you wouldn't take off."

His father chuckled ruefully and shook his head. "I know you act like it was easy, but the divorce was hard on you, too. Mom and I will always be here for you, and you'll always come first. So don't worry about Rebecca, okay? She'll come around. And if she doesn't, well…I'm not going anywhere. You, on the other hand, will grow up, go to college, and leave me and your mother all alone in this state." He faked a sob and covered his face with his hands.

Aaron laughed. "Dad! You're ridiculous."

He hadn't realized pressure had built on his shoulders, but at hearing his dad's words, the weight sitting there suddenly eased, and he took a deep breath. He trusted Dad. Everything would work out.

CHAPTER TWENTY

"No," his mother said as the three of them sat in the living room, the two adults with cups of coffee and Aaron with his hands jammed between his knees to keep them still.

"No?" Aaron questioned, his eyes widening. "But, Mom, I've got it all figured out and Dad said he would help."

"I did. I will give him the same amount I was going to give for the cat. The rest is up to him."

His mother stared at the two of them and sighed. "Richard. A dog is a lot more work. I'm not saying I have anything against Chance and his history. But what if he doesn't get along with Midnight?"

"He loves cats!" Aaron interjected. "He cuddles with them—it's the cutest thing."

"Okay, maybe he likes cats, but what if Midnight doesn't like him?"

"Midnight can get away if he doesn't want to play with him. He's always disappearing as it is."

His mother narrowed her eyes at him. "Aaron. Where is this dog going to stay while you're at school and I'm at work?"

"In a crate. I'll buy a big, strong one for him. Besides, we still have some time before school starts, so he can get used to it."

"Do you think it's fair to have a dog that spends seven hours a day in a crate?"

"We could start him in there and then let him out slowly to see what he does. Mom, if you're worried about him ruining things, I promise I'll replace anything he breaks. And it's not like we have many things he can break, anyway."

"What about the neighbors? Do you think they'll like us having a—"

"Who *cares* what the neighbors say! Mom, please! Did the neighbors care when Mr. Garrit's dog attacked me? Well…yes, I suppose, but did they suddenly think he was a beast? No. Half of them thought I'd done something to provoke the attack. We need to give Chance the opportunity to have a good life. He really likes me, Mom. Come see him while I'm working with him. I wanted to find him another home, and really, I tried, but he trusts me and I trust him. He's such a good dog."

"I'm not saying it's going to happen, but what if he turns and attacks someone?"

"Impossible. He's not going to be running loose."

"Nothing's impossible, Aaron. Look what happened to you."

Aaron sighed and hung his head, his fingers reaching up to run over his scars. "Mom, we have a fenced-in backyard. I'll buy a lead that he can stay on, so he's even limited in the backyard. I'll even buy something to reinforce the fence if you want me to. Please…I don't ask for much. I know our money situation is tight, and I promise you'll never have to pay a dime for him. I'll do all the work."

His mother stared at him and then at his father. "It's not that you're not responsible, Aaron. I know you are. When you say you'll do something, I have no doubt in my mind that you will. Dad and I raised you right despite going our separate ways. But you need to also think of the long term here. What happens when you go to college in two years? Chance can't go with you. You'll be busy with schoolwork, and I'll be stuck with him."

"There are plenty of good schools around here, Mom. I can still live at home and commute. It will save money not staying in a dorm."

For the first time in quite a while his father stepped in. "Son, I understand what your mother is saying, and to be honest, I regret not thinking of it first. Don't limit yourself because of Chance. If there's a school that interests you that's out of state you should go for it. Don't stay around here because of us or the dog."

"But I don't have an interest in going out of state! I never did."

"You're a sophomore," Mom argued. "How can you know that? You could change your mind next year. You don't even know what you want to major in yet. What if the schools around here don't offer the degree you want? You'll have no choice but to go out of state, or at the very least live on campus."

Aaron bit at his lip, his hands clasped between his knees to keep them from flying around to make his point. "I think I may have decided on what I'd like to do, actually. I was talking to Finn about it a while ago, and the idea kind of stuck."

"What's that?" his father asked, genuinely curious.

"I think maybe I'd like to teach history. There's so much out there to learn, and I like history already. Plus I'd be able to incorporate a lot of little-known facts to make it more interesting for kids. I think I could be good at it," he said. Aaron looked from his mom to his dad and back again. "And there are a lot of great colleges for teaching in the state. One of them close enough to be an easy commute, and not as expensive, either."

His mother sighed and dropped her head to her hands. "You're set on this, aren't you?"

"More than anything, Mom. I want Chance."

"Can you give me a few days to decide?"

Aaron beamed at her and nodded, feeling hopeful. "Yes, sure. Of course! Thank you."

"Wait, Aaron, I didn't say yes."

"I know, but you're at least considering it. That makes me happy." He got off his chair and threw his arms around her and his father. "Thank you both."

He left the two of them downstairs to talk. In his room, he flopped back on his bed and sent out a prayer that his mother accept his proposition. He knew he could take care of Chance if he was just given the opportunity to do so. Because if he couldn't adopt Chance himself, the dog's future looked grim.

CHAPTER TWENTY-ONE

Aaron got back from his job at the clothing store at four the next day. His body ached with the exhaustion from a long day dealing with parents and children looking for back-to-school clothes, but it had been worth it. He had gotten a few to open credit card accounts, and as a result, he would get a small bonus in his paycheck. His boss, Carl, had also told him he would need someone to stay on in the fall—because so many of the college students were going away—and offered him the position. He had accepted without question. Aaron figured he would deal with his mother and any of her displeasure later. He didn't want to tell his boss he would think about it only to have him offer it to someone else. And it would give him the opportunity to prove to his mother that he was responsible.

And get extra cash to take care of Chance, if he did adopt him.

When he got home, his mother still had not returned from her shift at the hospital. She had picked up extra hours that day because of a coworker, and she would be exhausted when she got home. To make it easier for her, Aaron got a pot of water and started it boiling. He pulled tomato sauce and spices out of the cabinet and started to make a spaghetti sauce with it. Once the water roiled he poured a little olive oil in it and then placed the pasta into the water. Letting that boil he turned his attention to the sauce.

His mother arrived home fifteen minutes later, and dinner sat ready on the table. Aaron heard her open the door. "Something smells wonderful!" she called out.

"I made pasta for dinner," he said, poking his head around the corner. "I hope that's all right."

"That's more than all right. I'm starving and exhausted. So glad I don't have to make dinner tonight, thank you."

"You're welcome."

Without another word she dumped her bags off her shoulder onto the floor. She joined Aaron at the table and the two ate in comfortable silence.

When he had eaten half of his plate, Aaron cleared his throat. "Carl offered me a permanent part-time position at the store today. A lot of the people there are leaving for college, and he's pretty impressed with my work. I told him I would take it."

His mother lowered her fork and frowned. "You agreed without talking to me?"

"I worried that if I said I needed to think about it I would lose the opportunity. Don't worry, Mom. I'll have fewer hours during the school year, and I promise if my grades drop I'll quit. But that's not going to happen."

She sighed but continued eating and nodded. "Fine. You're sixteen. But I'll have the final say in whether or not your grades have dropped."

"Deal," he said.

They continued their meal uninterrupted until his mother said, "Oh, and I forgot to tell you. I stopped by the shelter to talk to Maria today."

Aaron jerked his head up, splattering sauce on his shirt as his fork dropped. "You did? Why?"

"To look at Chance, of course."

"Do you mean…?" He could scarcely breathe. Tense moments passed before his mother reached into the pocket of her scrubs and handed him sheets of paper over the table.

"I suggest you fill it out very carefully and neatly. Without getting sauce all over it."

Aaron unfolded the papers and looked over the application for adoption. He had seen it before so many times, but now it seemed different.

"Mom…I don't know what to say…"

"For starters, *thank you* would be nice."

Aaron laughed and nearly lunged over the table to give her a hug. When his legs got tangled in the tablecloth as he stood, she held up her hand. "I get it. Just don't knock over the table."

"Thank you, Mom!"

"This isn't to say you'll be approved. I talked to Maria and she said you'll still have to go through the application process like everyone else and face an interview, but of course…the prospects do look good." She smiled knowingly.

"I'll fill it out as soon as I clean up and drop it off first thing tomorrow before work."

"I'll clean up tonight. You were sweet enough to cook for us, so as soon as you're done, go ahead and fill it out."

Aaron thanked her again and finished his food quickly. He barely tasted the sauce he had made as he inhaled the noodles. Strands whipped his face and splattered more sauce, making him look like he had regressed to being a five-year-old. His mother laughed, amused, and he wiped his face before kissing her cheek and dashing up the stairs to his room.

He hadn't thought she would decide so quickly. Maybe talking to Maria helped her decision. Whatever the case, he was thankful. Spreading the papers out and undoing the folds as best he could, he sat at his desk and pulled out a pen to fill out the four-page application. The first information was the easiest: name, date of birth, address, and work information. He filled it out quickly and moved to the rest. Though the rules said he must be twenty-one or older, he figured if his mother signed the application as well, it would be okay. And Maria wouldn't have given her the application if she didn't think it was fine.

The next information he had to look up. They wanted to know if he owned any other pets and the name of the veterinarian they went to. He listed all the details as well as he knew them. If he found someone else he would take Chance there, but for now Midnight's vet would do just as well.

He listed the name and breed of the dog he wanted—that was the easiest question for him, Chance, of course—and listed his reasons why. He had to write small because he nearly ran out of room. The questions that worried him the most were those about the daytime, when Chance would be left alone because of school and his mother being at work. He wrote as honestly as he could, after all Maria knew him well, and added that the dog would be crated until he had been in the house for a few months.

When he finished the paperwork, he brought it downstairs for his mother to look over. She read it carefully and nodded. "It all looks good."

"What about the part that says I need to be twenty-one?" he asked. "I mean, Maria knows I'm only sixteen, so it has to be okay, right?"

His mother smiled faintly. "Well, you do need to be of age to adopt, but I filled out a bit of paperwork myself." When Aaron stared at her blankly, she continued. "I wanted you to do the paperwork yourself. He is going to be your dog, and you will be responsible for him. But Maria cannot bend the rules for anyone who works there. She has my paperwork on file, but she is waiting for yours to come in as well before she begins her reference checks."

"Have I ever told you that you're the best mom ever?" Aaron asked seriously.

"Once or twice," she replied with a wink.

Aaron had to work at ten, but he arrived at the shelter promptly at eight to drop off his paperwork. He found Maria in the dog kennels, cleaning out any overnight accidents and giving the dogs their breakfast and water.

"Maria?" he asked, not wanting to disturb her but needing her attention.

She looked up from one of the kennels and smiled. "Ah, Aaron. I kind of expected I'd see you early this morning. I take it you got the paperwork filled out?"

"Yes, ma'am. Mom told me she filled out a set, as well."

"She did, yes. You can't officially adopt an animal until you're twenty-one, so your mother will technically—if the paperwork goes through—be the one the dog goes to, but we understand the situation very well."

"Did you want me to leave the papers on your desk, or…?" he trailed off.

"Let me finish up in here—I'm almost done. And then we'll get the interview out of the way unless you need to be at work soon?"

"I don't work until ten."

"Great," she said. "Meet me in the office, then, and I'll talk to you and look over the application."

Aaron left the room and took a seat in her office. His leg bounced with energy as he waited fifteen minutes for her to finish up and join him. By the time she came in, the paper had wrinkled a bit in his hands. He set it on her desk before she could sit and wiped the palms of his hands on his jeans.

"I remember the first day you came into my office, over three months ago. You were just as nervous," she teased as she took her own seat.

"I remember that like it was yesterday."

"It practically was," she said as she picked up the application. Another one sat ready on the side of her desk—likely his mother's—and she slid it over to compare them. She took a few minutes to look them over, nodding and making soft noises as she did so. When she finished, she slid a yellow legal pad over in front of her, picked up a pen, and started talking.

"Why do you want to adopt Chance?" she asked bluntly.

Aaron was taken aback by the question and it took him a moment to gather his thoughts. "I want to give Chance the opportunity to have a good home. I've grown attached to him working here."

"There are many animals you'll grow attached to when you work in a shelter. You experienced that yourself when you first started, with a particular kitten. What makes Chance different?"

Aaron bit his lip, trying not to be intimidated by the questions. Would his quick attachment to Little Dipper affect her decision? "Chance is like me. He's scarred and he was scared when he came in here. We're both still scarred, but we're no longer scared. I am afraid, though, that his time is running out, and he's such a sweet dog and deserves a good life. I can provide that for him."

Maria nodded and jotted down notes.

"I do like a lot of the animals here, but Chance is the one that has helped me overcome my fear of dogs. I worked with him the most, and because he helped me, I want to help him, too. I feel like I can go anywhere unafraid now, and it's all because of him."

"Do you have a way to pay for the dog?" she asked.

"Yes. My boss offered me a permanent part-time position at the store. It's not much, but I've been saving my money this summer, and my father has agreed to help pay for some of the vet costs."

Maria nodded again and wrote this down as well. "As you know, all dogs and cats that leave here—if they are of age—are spayed or neutered, up to date on shots, and given a microchip implant. This is all part of the adoption package at no extra charge. Before he leaves he will be examined by our veterinarian, but I suggest you take him to your own vet as well so they can get to know him."

Aaron nodded. None of this was new to him. "Does that mean…?"

"I still need to go over your references. If they check out…" She smiled.

Breathing a sigh of relief, he stood and held out his hand. "Thank you, Maria."

"I have no doubt everything will check out. I'll let you know in a few days."

A few days? Aaron nearly screamed his frustration. He had expected it to take just a day, but he forced himself to stay calm and nodded. "I look forward to hearing from you."

CHAPTER TWENTY-TWO

Aaron didn't hear from Maria or anyone else at the shelter. He started to worry. Part of him wanted to go out to buy supplies for Chance, but another part of him feared someone else would—at the last minute—put in an application for him, someone who could better care for him.

"Relax," Mom told him. "If it's meant to be, it will all work out in the end."

"Don't worry about it, buddy," Dad said. "You'll get him. Look at how much work you've put in with him."

Even Rebecca joined the chorus. "Let me know when you get him home! I'd love to visit and see him, if it's all right with your mother." Despite his initial caution about the woman and her reaction to his being gay, she'd turned around quickly and seemed to accept it as a part of him. He welcomed the relief it offered. Dad had been right about her just needing a little time.

It was perfectly fine, according to his mother. But Aaron still worried that something was going on. On Thursday night, he called Finn to vent.

"What's taking so long?" he whined. He lay in his bed, the book on dog training propped up against his raised legs.

"Well, there are many factors. Maybe your references aren't available to talk to Maria yet," Finn answered calmly. Aaron could hear the sound of clanking dishes in the background and assumed he was washing them.

"My references have been home all week, or I made sure to give their work numbers."

"Calm down, Aaron. It's not a big deal. Maria might have a lot of other adoption paperwork to go through. She has a lot of work as a director. And don't forget, she does have days off, too. Even though she always seems to be there, she's not."

Aaron sighed and tossed the book onto the floor. "I just don't know if I should go out and buy things for him yet, or wait."

"You could always return the things if you find out you don't need them."

"True," Aaron replied, not having thought of that. "I've never had a dog before. It's always been cats, so I know what to buy for Midnight, but I don't want to go overboard buying useless things for Chance…if I get him. Will you go with me to the store?"

"Yeah, we can go tomorrow after work if you'll drive me there and back to the shelter. I'm a little low on gas and I don't get paid until next week."

"I'll come pick you up tomorrow, then. That'll make it easier." It didn't, really. It would mean he would have to get up earlier to get to Finn's house and it would take him out of his way, but he would do it for his friend.

"Really? That would be great," Finn said, sounding relieved.

"Sure. I'll come get you by nine."

"Excellent. See you then."

When Aaron arrived to pick Finn up at his apartment, he already sat outside waiting on the steps of his building. He didn't even have to put the car in park before Finn had the door open and the seat belt on.

"Bad morning?" Aaron asked, not sure if he wanted to hear the answer, not because he didn't care, but because he cared almost too much. He hated knowing Finn's miserable situation.

"They're not awake yet. I just wanted to be sure I was out before they were up."

Aaron nodded and turned the car around toward the shelter.

"So I think the place with the best, most affordable supplies is near the mall. Still up for that?" Finn asked.

"Sounds like a plan."

"Great," Finn said, and he pulled a list out of his pocket. "I hope you don't mind, but I made a list of things you'll definitely need, and other things you might find useful but might not want to get right now."

Aaron laughed and stopped at the light as it turned red. "If you have a book on dog training on there, check that one off. I bought the one at your bookstore."

"I remember that." Finn snorted. "You're going to need dog food—a big bag for him, and I'll help you select the best quality brand—a dog bed, a large enough crate for him, two dog bowls, preferably stainless steel, some toys, and some treats. Oh, and you'll definitely want this spray that cleans messes out of carpets and leaves no smell behind. That's more necessary than the dog bed."

Aaron listened as Finn listed the things and mentally checked off how much money he had access to in his debit account. He hoped it would be enough for all these items. The last thing he wanted was to get Chance and then find out he really couldn't afford to take care of him.

They arrived at the shelter a little before their shift, and as soon as they entered the entire building seemed to buzz with excitement. Both boys looked at Sandra who smiled brightly when they entered. Normally she was busy working and only looked up briefly, but she held their gaze for much longer than usual and asked how their day was going.

"It just started," Finn joked, ushering Aaron toward the staff room. "I'll keep you updated as it goes."

The door to the room had been left shut, but when they tried to open it, they found it locked. "Well, that's bizarre," Aaron said, giving the handle another twist and shove.

"I'll go get the key from Sandra. She has a spare." Finn turned back the way they came, leaving Aaron standing at the door. He could hear movement inside and he wondered if someone had just shut the door behind them to make a private call and accidentally locked it.

He knocked. "Can you open the door?"

Finn returned with the key. "Who are you talking to?"

"I don't know," he admitted. "I heard someone moving around inside."

"Well," Finn said, making a face, "let's hope it's not two people in an awkward position."

Aaron widened his eyes. "At an animal shelter?"

"You never know." He knocked as well and called out that he had the key and was opening the door. The key twisted in the door and he pushed it open, but they couldn't see anyone. The shades were drawn and the lights stayed off, despite a sensor.

"Let's shed a little light on the situation," Aaron said as he stepped into the room behind Finn. As he flicked on the light, the source of movement became clear and started to whine from inside a large crate. "Chance!"

Sitting inside a large black crate was Chance. He wiggled around, whining and trying to get out. On the crate was a big red bow.

"Well, I guess we know what that means," Finn said, grinning.

"Congratulations!" Maria cried from behind them. The boys spun to face her, and Aaron couldn't help himself as he threw his arms around her tightly.

"Thank you!"

She laughed and eased out of his grip. "He's been in there for half an hour and probably wants to see you. Go let him out."

Aaron complied and rushed across the room to free Chance from the crate. The pit bull clambered out and knocked Aaron over, slobbering his face in excitement. Aaron wondered if he could sense what was going on; he had never before knocked anyone over no matter how excited he became.

"We knew yesterday that he would be going home with you, but we wanted to make it a surprise for when you came in today," Amy said. When Aaron turned, he saw that she had joined Maria at the door. "We all pitched in and bought you a sturdy crate for him."

Tears formed in Aaron's eyes and he blinked them back. "Thank you so much. I don't know how I can repay you."

"Just keep doing what you're doing," Maria said, smiling. "That's all the payment we need."

"There is one minor thing, though," Amy said, glancing at Maria. "Chance can't go home until Sunday. Our vet is out of town until then, but he agreed to stop in as soon as he came back. We were going to wait until Sunday to tell you about Chance, but we figured you would need some time to get the house ready, too."

Though disappointment flooded through him with the news Chance wouldn't be going home with him that day, he was grateful for the opportunity to get everything ready. "That's great, thank you. Finn and I are going to the store after work to pick up some things."

"So you figured it out?" Maria asked.

Aaron flushed and shook his head. "Not exactly. Finn just thought I could buy what I needed and return it if things didn't work out."

Inclining her head toward Finn, she agreed. "That was a decent plan. But now you won't need to take anything back."

Aaron turned and stared at Chance who had his head butted against his leg. His tail wagged excitedly, and Aaron smiled as he stroked his broad head.

"I suggest you enroll him in obedience classes. There's a local trainer that I can get you in touch with that teaches Canine Good Citizen classes. That would be great for him."

"That would be excellent, thank you," Aaron said, still looking down at his dog. *His* dog. He never thought he would say those words, never in a million years. But Chance had changed all of that. He couldn't wait to bring him home on Sunday.

❖

After work, Aaron and Finn made their way to the pet store. On his break, he had called his mom and told her the good news, then called his dad and Rebecca. Until he could go home, Chance stayed comfortable in his old kennel, spending a few final days playing with the friends he'd made at the shelter.

The pet store was huge, and without Finn, Aaron would have felt lost. There were so many cool things he wanted to buy, but Finn assured him not all of them were necessary. They grabbed a cart and made their way around the store. They picked out a large pillow bed for Chance to sleep on, and another for his crate, to make it more comfortable when he had to be locked inside. Because he was a larger dog, they also bought him a harness to use when he went on walks, which Finn said would prevent him from pulling. They got a reflective leash, and Finn made sure he got the healthiest food Aaron could afford.

Maria had said Chance would be going home with the toys he loved so much, but Aaron bought a few more, as well as a box of small treats to keep up his training. They picked out sturdy dog bowls, and when Aaron thought he was done, Finn directed him toward another section.

"You're going to need to groom him, too. Even though his fur is short, you'll still need to keep him clean." They grabbed shampoo, a soft brush, nail clippers, and some sort of cleaner that would remove stains and odors from the carpet.

When they went to ring up everything, Aaron was pleased to find himself well under budget. He breathed a sigh of relief as he swiped the debit card and put in his pin number.

Together the two managed to get everything in the trunk of his car, and then Aaron headed toward Finn's apartment.

"I just realized…is Chance going to fit in his crate in the backseat?" Finn asked, glancing behind him.

"He'll fit. I can bring the back seats down so that the whole back is open to the trunk."

"Oh. Cool. Then yeah, that should be no problem. Do you want me to come over Sunday after work to help you settle Chance in?"

"I'd like that, but do you think it will be too many people? I don't want to overwhelm him and make him nervous."

"He knows the two of us. He'll really only have to get used to your mother and your cat, and I'm sure Midnight will make himself scarce."

"Okay, then yes. I'd love it if you were there."

"Great. You should limit him to one room for the first few days so he gets used to it. This will be a very new situation for him."

Aaron nodded and pulled up outside Finn's building. "Hey, thanks for everything, Finn."

Finn shrugged. "What are friends for?"

When Finn hesitated and glanced up at the building, Aaron reached out and rested a hand on his shoulder. "Hey, it's going to be okay."

"I know. Just one more year and I'm out."

"You'll always have a way out. You can come stay with me and Mom."

"What?" Finn jerked back and stared at Aaron.

"I'm sure she wouldn't mind."

"I couldn't do that. That's asking too much." Finn sighed and offered a smile. "But thanks. It's nice knowing I have a backup. Just in case." He looked up one more time. "I think it'll be different for now, though. The fighting has gotten less severe. Maybe they're... changing."

Aaron didn't want to negate Finn's optimism, but he hoped he was right, for his friend's sake.

Finn climbed out of the car and they said good-bye. With one last glance backward at Finn, Aaron turned toward home.

His mother had already gotten home from work, and dinner waited on the table. She helped Aaron unload the car, and for the moment, they placed everything in the living room. After they ate dinner, the two of them sat in the middle of the pile of stuff.

"So where is his crate going to go?" she asked, looking around.

"By the back door, I think. It's quieter back there, and when we come home he won't be instantly bombarded by us."

His mother nodded approval. "We can put this pillow here in the living room so he can lie down while we're watching TV. And I have an old basket we can use to put his toys in. I don't want them scattered all over the place. And even though he has short fur, we'll have to do more cleaning around the house. I'm sure he's going to shed something awful. But...we'll deal with that. And hopefully Midnight won't mind sharing his space."

"Once he gets used to Chance, he'll be fine. If I can overcome my fears, Midnight can get over his."

Mom smiled proudly at him, reaching over and patting his leg. "Greater miracles have happened. Let's see what Sunday brings."

CHAPTER TWENTY-THREE

Aaron thought Sunday evening would never arrive. He worked a full shift Saturday, which seemed longer than usual. Sunday's work hours dragged even more. It seemed like every time he looked at the clock, the hands slowed or went backward. At one point, he rubbed his eyes, approached the clock, and listened for the soft tick, convinced the battery had died.

"You know," Finn said as they sat outside and let some of the larger dogs stretch their legs, "a watched pot never boils."

"What's that supposed to mean?"

"It means that the more you look at the clock, the slower time will seem to pass. Don't worry about it. Four will get here soon enough, and then we'll bring Chance home."

"Do you think he'll like it?"

"Are you kidding? He'll love it. Just make sure you take him straight outside when you get there so he doesn't get so excited he pees on the carpet. I'm sure your mom won't appreciate that as his first greeting."

Aaron laughed, shaking his head. "Yeah, no. Not really."

At a quarter to four, volunteers who had the day off arrived to say good-bye to Chance. Even though Aaron promised to bring him in and bring pictures all the time, some of them were leaving for college and might not be back the next year. Even Amy stopped in, although it was her day off.

Finn offered to load the crate in the car while Aaron got Chance ready to say good-bye. He clipped his new leash onto the collar he had bought him and attached the nametag Savannah had given as a gift, earlier that day. With his lips pulled back in a canine grin, Chance looked like he'd just won the doggy Lotto. The vet had stopped in that morning and given him a clean bill of health, declaring him free to go.

The staff lined the kennels as Aaron led him proudly out to the front. Some of them clapped and others knelt down, interrupting the walk, to give Chance a pat or a hug. He ate up the attention, slobbering affection on anyone who got close enough.

"Take care of him," Savannah said with a smile.

"Of course," Aaron said as they passed the last staff member. Sandra said good-bye at the door and gave Chance a cookie, which he inhaled. His tail whipped back and forth, slapping hard against Aaron's leg.

Finn leaned against his car with the door open. The crate sat inside and had plenty of room. When Chance saw the open door, he barked and pulled at his leash, wanting to get in. It surprised Aaron; the last time he had been in a car was on his trip over, with Officer Hardy.

"I'll toss a treat into the crate when he gets in the car to lure him into it," Finn said, and Aaron agreed. He left the leash on and laughed as Chance struggled to pick his back legs up. In the end, they had to boost him into the car. He didn't want to get into the crate at first, but after Finn tossed the treat in, he dove after it. They locked the gate after him and he settled down, his ears perked forward with interest.

Aaron worried how Chance would take the drive in the car; he'd heard horror stories of dogs being carsick and making a mess, but he didn't have to worry. The hum of the tires on the road seemed to lull Chance, and when they stopped at their first light, Aaron glanced back to find Chance nearly asleep.

They made it home without incident, though Aaron did drive more carefully than usual. Mom was sitting on the front steps waiting for them when they arrived. The minute Aaron put the car in park and shut down the engine, Chance woke, and his tail started banging against the side of the cage.

Aaron opened the cage and quickly grabbed Chance's leash. The dog tried to burst from the car and run for his mother, but he asked him to heel and Chance stayed at his side. He still wiggled with energy, but at least he listened. Finn unloaded the crate and carried it behind Aaron. When they approached his mother, Aaron told Chance to sit. The dog listened at first, but his butt kept trying to leave the ground.

His mother walked over slowly, hand out, to let Chance sniff her. When he tried to jump up on her, Aaron firmly said, "Down." Chance whined but sat again, lifting first one foot then the other in a sort of dance.

"His training went well," Finn said as he placed the kennel on the porch. "But you'll have to work hard to reinforce it."

Aaron nodded and reached into his pocket, pulling out a treat. Chance instantly focused on him and stared at the hand. "Good sit," he told him before giving him the treat.

"He certainly is a bundle of energy," his mother remarked as she stroked his head. "But I'm sure he'll settle down. Let's bring him in and let him explore the living room. I have the stairs blocked off, and Midnight is shut in my room."

Walking ahead of the boys, his mother opened the door. Keeping him on the leash, Aaron walked through the living room to the back sliding-glass door. "I think I'll take him out first, Mom. That way he won't mess up the carpet."

Opening the door, he led Chance out. The gates were closed and locked, so Aaron figured it would be safe to let him go free. He left the leash on in case he needed to grab him but dropped it from his hand.

Chance crept about the yard, sniffing everything within sight. He relieved himself on a couple of bushes they had around the yard, effectively marking his territory, and continued snooping. Aaron sat on the steps, and soon Finn and his mother joined him.

"He looks pretty pleased with himself," Finn remarked as Chance ran from one side of the yard to the other. His mother brought out a new ball and tossed it to him. He chased it down and then flopped onto his stomach and gnawed on it.

"I think he's going to be very happy here," Mom added, smiling as she wrapped an arm around Aaron's shoulder.

When Chance looked calm and had played with his new ball for a while, Aaron grabbed his leash and led him inside. Finn set the crate up by the back door where he could have a view of the yard or not, depending on whether or not the curtains were closed. His mother set the food and water bowls on a mat in the kitchen, to keep the mess to a minimum. Chance's pillow bed had already been set up in the living room next to an old wicker basket filled with toys. His mom had even found an old blanket she thought he might enjoy and had tossed it onto the bed.

Holding onto the leash, Aaron let Chance explore and followed behind him. He sniffed every surface available, sometimes lifting his head and sniffing the air. When he got to the pillow, he stepped on it, turned around in a circle, and sank onto the soft surface.

"Well, he definitely knows that's his bed!" Mom laughed.

Aaron unclipped the leash and Chance stayed in his spot. Finn and his mother joined him on the couch and watched him.

"I'll call the vet tomorrow and set up his first checkup, " Aaron said.

"You know Tyler is going to want to come over and visit him, and probably Caleb, too. And your father and Rebecca asked to come."

At the mention of Caleb, Aaron frowned. "I'm not sure I want Caleb over for a while. Not after what he did to Will. Not until he apologizes to him for it."

"What if he doesn't?" Mom asked.

"Then…that's his business." Once he'd said it, the truth of it struck him, clear as crystal—he knew he'd be okay with losing Caleb as a friend. Because, what was a *friend,* anyway? Certainly not Caleb. Aaron knew he had Finn, after all, and everyone else at the shelter. There would be a million people in his future who would accept him and befriend him—love him—differences and scars and all. Caleb, and all he represented, was his past. Why hadn't he seen it sooner?

"If Dad calls while you're out, when should I tell him to stop over?"

Aaron shook his head and cleared his thoughts, focusing on the present. "Next week. I think he needs time to get used to the house and us first. After that, they can visit."

"You should set him up with obedience classes, too, like Maria said. I think that will help strengthen what he already knows for commands," Finn said.

"Do you know the person Maria recommends?"

Finn grinned. "Of course I do. Lorraine Alger. She's great—she used to volunteer at the shelter before I was there. Now she runs obedience classes that will get you a Canine Good Citizen certificate. It's an excellent thing to have, and it will show everyone that Chance is a fantastic dog."

Aaron nodded. "I like the sound of that. Could you get me her number?"

"Absolutely. I'll text it to you when I find it. She only takes a limited number of dogs at a time, though, so make sure you call her right away and see if a class is open."

"I'll call her first thing in the morning, before work."

With Chance settled down and his mother comfortable, Aaron offered to take Finn home. On the ride, he thanked him for all the help he had given him.

Finn laughed. "I feel like we've already had this conversation. Look, it's nothing. We're friends, right? I'm glad you got Chance. You're the best thing that's happened to him, and I think he's the best thing that's happened to you."

It was hard to disagree with him, though Aaron wanted to add that meeting Finn topped even the amazingness of Chance. But he held back. He said good-bye as Finn climbed out of the car. While he drove home he thought of all the changes that had taken place over the last few months. He'd gotten over his fear of dogs and had adopted a rescue, his father was dating, his friends had apologized—well, at least one of them had—and he'd made another, even better friend. Life definitely looked good.

CHAPTER TWENTY-FOUR

Chance quickly acclimated to his new home. Within days he had the run of the house while they were home, and enjoyed the life of luxury. Every morning, Aaron took him for a long walk. When he got home from work he took him for another walk around the neighborhood. And before bed they wandered through town, which left both of them exhausted. In between all of that he played, slept, and made friends with Midnight, who did come around. When it became clear to Midnight that Chance wouldn't hurt him, the elusive cat began to appear more and more often.

Aaron called Lorraine Alger, but her current class was full. She did have an opening in the new session that began the week school started, so Aaron enrolled him in that class. Chance's new vet gave him another clean bill of health and sent him home with a bag of treats and goodies. Dad and Rebecca had stopped by to visit, and Rebecca gushed over what a good dog he was.

He was surprised by how well Mom got along with her. Aaron thought for sure his dad's new girlfriend being in their house would cause awkward tension, but instead she greeted Rebecca as if she were a long-lost friend.

Sometimes adults surprised him.

Tyler liked Chance, too, and he often came over just for the excuse of having the dog lounge with them on the couch. Once they went out toward the pond and met up with Will and his dog for a walk, but both dogs wanted to play more than anything. For Chance it was a plus, but at the same time it exhausted the boys, and they did very little walking.

"Chance is doing great," Will said, letting his boxer pull him forward. "Alfie, no."

"Ever think you'd see Aaron walking a dog?" Tyler laughed. Aaron reached out to cuff his shoulder, but he moved out of range and Chance barked excitedly, interpreting the quick moves as play.

"I didn't really know Aaron before Chance. I mean, we knew each other from GSA, but we didn't hang out. I knew he didn't like dogs, but I'd never seen him around them anyway."

"Well," Tyler said once he was safely on Will's other side, "you wouldn't believe how different he is now. You'd never know!"

"That's good, right?" Will asked.

"Of course." Aaron snorted. "Why wouldn't it be?"

The three managed to finish a lap around the pond, letting the dogs play in the water briefly, before they reached the far side and the parking lot. There were a few cars parked in the shade. One of them belonged to Caleb.

"Oh no," Will said, recognizing him as he climbed out of the driver's seat.

"Don't worry about it," Aaron said, standing next to him. "He's not going to say anything, and if he does, we'll deal with it."

"I don't want any trouble."

"There won't be," Tyler added. He looked at Will. "I'm sorry about what he did to your locker at the end of the year. I didn't think he'd be such a dick." When Will just shrugged, Tyler nudged him. "Hey, don't worry about it. I've got your back."

Will looked up in surprise, and Aaron couldn't hold back the smile from his face. Tyler friends with one of the guys from GSA?

Yeah, life was good.

Now if only he could find a boyfriend.

❖

It wasn't long before summer ended and Aaron went back to school. His boss gave him the first week off, and because of Chance's obedience classes, his working schedule changed. After school he would work Monday, Tuesday, and Friday, leaving him Wednesday to do schoolwork and Thursday for Chance's classes.

He could only volunteer on the weekends, but Maria had agreed to that arrangement.

The first week of classes was short—school started on Wednesday—so Aaron got the opportunity to spend a little more time with Chance before the schedule they had established changed. Once school started, he worried Chance would be bored, but when he got home from school on Wednesday he found his dog sound asleep in his crate with no mess to pick up.

Thursday was the day.

Aaron got home from school, did some of his homework, ate a quick dinner, and then took Chance for a long walk around the neighborhood to get rid of any excess energy before the class.

When they got back, Chance looked like he wanted to lie down—they had walked longer than usual—but Aaron loaded him in his car. Chance quickly settled into the backseat on a folded blanket and stared out the window as Aaron drove.

Lorraine had given him the address of her home when he'd called to set up the classes. It took twenty minutes to get there, and Aaron arrived with a few minutes to spare. Because they were going to be around quite a few other dogs with varying temperaments, he'd brought Chance's harness, just in case. When he arrived, he parked in the street.

The house before him was a large single-floor ranch, with a yard enclosed by a tall chain-link fence. A few other cars were parked on the street and one in the driveway. Aaron got out and opened the back door, grasping Chance's leash before he could get out and take off.

Asking him to heel, the two made it to the front door without incident. Worried about ringing the bell and setting off a loud chorus of barking, Aaron knocked instead. A few moments later, a middle-aged woman answered the door with a smile. She glanced down at Chance and nodded. "You must be Aaron and Chance, then."

"How did you know?"

The woman laughed. "I only have one pit bull in class this time around. Come on in. We're in the backyard," she said.

Lorraine was a tall thin woman with light brown hair pulled back in a ponytail. She wore jeans and an old T-shirt. As they walked through the living room to the back door, Aaron could see Lorraine loved dogs; decorating nearly every available surface were pictures, statues, or other memorabilia featuring dogs.

The spacious backyard had one section filled with sand and another outfitted with a series of ramps and jumps for dogs to play on. Chance perked up when he saw those and started to tug his way over, but Aaron held onto him firmly.

Toward the center of the yard, a group of people stood with their dogs sniffing each other. There were seven people in the class altogether and seven dogs. As Lorraine had told him, Chance was the only pit bull. An older woman held on to the leash of a long, sad-looking bassett hound. A teen boy about his age held on to the leash of a young German shepherd. There was also a young Akita, a beagle, and two Rottweilers.

"Well, we're all here," Lorraine said as she moved to the group. "I like to start with introductions first, because for the next few months all of you will be classmates. Your dogs will get to know each other, you will get to know each other, and hopefully at the end of the classes, all of your dogs will graduate together and get their Canine Good Citizen certificates. If you wanted to continue on and get your dog certified for therapy or rescue work, I can give you more information on that individually. Some dogs are suitable for work and others aren't. But again, we can talk about those particulars later.

"As you know since you signed up for my class, my name is Lorraine Alger. I was a math teacher and volunteered at the Happy Endings Animal Foundation for a few years, where I discovered that I needed a change. I quit my job as a teacher and worked to get a master's degree in animal science. I now teach yet again, but this time it's animal science at a vocational agricultural high school. I'm also a certified canine massage therapist. Unfortunately, I've had to stop working at the shelter, but I do foster dogs for them when my own home isn't practically a literal zoo." She smiled warmly when she said this and looked around the group for a volunteer to go next.

The older woman's name was Carmen, and her dog, the bassett hound, was Sherlock. The owners of the Rottweilers, Brendan and Meagan, were a dating couple who had rescued their dogs Kylie and Cyrus. The white Akita, Yuki, belonged to Jason, who looked familiar to Aaron. When he announced he worked at the pet store Aaron and

Finn had been to a few weeks before, it clicked. *That's why he looks so familiar. He rang us up!* Aaron nodded his head toward him. Jason returned the smile with a grin that reached up to his eyes. The beagle, Rascal, could hardly sit still, and the woman holding on to his leash could barely tell them her name was Susan before he nearly broke free.

"Oh my, looks like we have an excitable pup with this one!" Lorraine exclaimed with a short laugh.

"I'm so sorry," Susan said. "I should have brought him to classes before, but I kept putting it off. I'm almost afraid it's too late, now."

"It's never too late, trust me. You just need to be firm with him and offer lots of positive reinforcement. We'll get him straightened out in no time."

Susan looked relieved and bent down to hold onto Rascal more firmly. He was eying Yuki and looked like he wanted to play or chew his tail—Aaron wasn't sure which.

The introductions finally got to the teen with the German shepherd, and Aaron glanced at him. He was tall and lanky with black hair that spiked up in front, away from his eyes, unlike the hair that Aaron hid behind. When he looked at him, Aaron found him staring back and he felt his face flush. He gave Aaron a shy smile and glanced down at his dog.

"My name is Nikolai, but everyone just calls me Niko. And this is my dog, Dante. We've always had German shepherds when I was growing up, and after our older dog passed last year, I saved up to get my own."

"Welcome to the group, Niko. Dante already looks like he's been through some training," Lorraine said, clearly impressed.

Niko shrugged. "I taught him how to sit, stay, and lie down."

"It's a great start. He's already ahead of the class and can be a good role model for the other dogs. Speaking of well-behaved dogs, Chance looks like he's had quite a bit of training, as well."

Aaron nodded and realized it was his turns for introductions. "I'm Aaron, and this is Chance."

"He's a pit bull," Carmen said, looking skeptical. But Aaron held his ground and nodded proudly.

"He is. An American pit bull terrier, to be exact. He's a rescue from the Happy Endings Animal Foundation. He was brought in shortly after I started volunteering there, when animal control found him abandoned in a lot. They suspect that he was used as a bait dog, but he's the best dog and he's very people-friendly."

Lorraine smiled and rested a hand on his shoulder. "One thing we can learn in class is all about the different breeds represented here. They're very diverse, just like their owners. And they all have something unique to offer."

Aaron glanced over toward Niko and found him looking at him again. He offered him a smile and Niko returned it, his gaze taking him in from top to bottom. His eyes didn't even linger on the scars like everyone else's had, and Aaron knew he was blushing again.

Hmmm…

If luck was on his side, maybe Aaron would learn a thing or two from this class, as well.

About the Author

While growing up, Jennifer Lavoie wanted to be a writer or a teacher and briefly debated a career in marine biology. The only problem with that was her fear of deep water. Starting during a holiday season as temporary help, she worked in a bookstore for six years and made it all the way up to assistant manager before she left to take a job teaching. Jennifer has her bachelor's degree in secondary English education and found her first teaching job working with middle school students. Along with another teacher and a handful of students, Jennifer started the first Gay-Straight Alliance at the school. She has since moved to another school, but is still active in student clubs and enjoys pairing students with books that make them love to read. Jennifer lives in Connecticut with her cat, Scout.

Soliloquy Titles From Bold Strokes Books

Meeting Chance by Jennifer Lavoie. When man's best friend turns on Aaron Cassidy, the teen keeps his distance until fate puts Chance in his hands. (978-1-60282-952-7)

Asher's Fault by Elizabeth Wheeler. Fourteen-year-old Asher Price sees the world in black and white, much like the photos he takes, but when his little brother drowns at the same moment Asher experiences his first same-sex kiss, he can no longer hide behind the lens of his camera and eventually discovers he isn't the only one with a secret. (978-1-60282-982-4)

Lake Thirteen by Greg Herren. A visit to an old cemetery seems like fun to a group of five teenagers, who soon learn that sometimes it's best to leave old ghosts alone. (978-1-60282-894-0)

The Road to Her by KE Payne. Sparks fly when actress Holly Croft, star of UK soap Portobello Road, meets her new on-screen love interest, the enigmatic and sexy Elise Manford. (978-1-60282-887-2)

Kings of Ruin by Sam Cameron. High school student Danny Kelly and loner Kevin Clark must team up to defeat a top-secret alien intelligence that likes to wreak havoc with fiery car, truck, and train accidents. (978-1-60282-864-3)

Swans & Klons by Nora Olsen. In a future world where there are no males, sixteen-year-old Rubric and her girlfriend Salmon Jo must fight to survive when everything they believed in turns out to be a lie. (978-1-60282-874-2)

The You Know Who Girls by Annameekee Hesik. As they begin freshman year, Abbey Brooks and her best friend, Kate, pinky swear they'll keep away from the lesbians in Gila High, but Abbey already suspects she's one of those you-know-who girls herself and slowly learns who her true friends really are. (978-1-60282-754-7)

In Stone by Jeremy Jordan King. A young New Yorker is rescued from a hate crime by a mysterious someone who turns out to be more of a something. (978-1-60282-761-5)

Wonderland by David-Matthew Barnes. After her mother's sudden death, Destiny Moore is sent to live with her two gay uncles on Avalon Cove, a mysterious island on which she uncovers a secret place called Wonderland, where love and magic prove to be real. (978-1-60282-788-2)

Another 365 Days by KE Payne. Clemmie Atkins is back, and her life is more complicated than ever! Still madly in love with her girlfriend, Clemmie suddenly finds her life turned upside down with distractions, confessions, and the return of a familiar face... (978-1-60282-775-2)

The Secret of Othello by Sam Cameron. Florida teen detectives Steven and Denny risk their lives to search for a sunken NASA satellite—but under the waves, no one can hear you scream... (978-1-60282-742-4)

Andy Squared by Jennifer Lavoie. Andrew never thought anyone could come between him and his twin sister, Andrea...until Ryder rode into town. (978-1-60282-743-1)

Sara by Greg Herren. A mysterious and beautiful new student at Southern Heights High School stirs things up when students start dying. (978-1-60282-674-8)

Boys of Summer, edited by Steve Berman. Stories of young love and adventure, when the sky's ceiling is a bright blue marvel, when another boy's laughter at the beach can distract from dull summer jobs. (978-1-60282-663-2)

Street Dreams by Tama Wise. Tyson Rua has more than his fair share of problems growing up in New Zealand—he's gay, he's falling in love, and he's run afoul of the local hip-hop crew leader just as he's trying to make it as a graffiti artist. (978-1-60282-650-2)

me@you.com by KE Payne. Is it possible to fall in love with someone you've never met? Imogen Summers thinks so because it's happened to her. (978-1-60282-592-5)

Swimming to Chicago by David-Matthew Barnes. As the lives of the adults around them unravel, high school students Alex and Robby form an unbreakable bond, vowing to do anything to stay together—even if it means leaving everything behind. (978-1-60282-572-7)

365 Days by KE Payne. Life sucks when you're seventeen years old and confused about your sexuality, and the girl of your dreams doesn't even know you exist. Then in walks sexy new emo girl, Hannah Harrison. Clemmie Atkins has exactly 365 days to discover herself, and she's going to have a blast doing it! (978-1-60282-540-6)

Cursebusters! by Julie Smith. Budding psychic Reeno is the most accomplished teenage burglar in California, but one tiny screw-up and poof!—she's sentenced to Bad Girl School. And that isn't even her worst problem. Her sister Haley's dying of an illness no one can diagnose, and now she can't even help. (978-1-60282-559-8)

Who I Am by M.L. Rice. Devin Kelly's senior year is a disaster. She's in a new school in a new town, and the school bully is making her life miserable—but then she meets his sister Melanie and realizes her feelings for her are more than platonic. (978-1-60282-231-3)

Sleeping Angel by Greg Herren. Eric Matthews survives a terrible car accident only to find out everyone in town thinks he's a murderer—and he has to clear his name even though he has no memories of what happened. (978-1-60282-214-6)

Mesmerized by David-Matthew Barnes. Through her close friendship with Brodie and Lance, Serena Albright learns about the many forms of love and finds comfort for the grief and guilt she feels over the brutal death of her older brother, the victim of a hate crime. (978-1-60282-191-0)